Susquehanna Valley

ISBN: 1-4700-3225-2
ISBN-13: 9781470032258

Susquehanna Valley

Thomas Schappert

2012

I would like to sincerely thank Amanda Hrycyna of The Wyoming Valley, Pennsylvania, for making the beautiful image on the cover. I am grateful and glad for anyone who grows to understand how perfect it works with this collection of short fiction.

CONTENTS

Flying Solo

John walked onto Mr. Hanlon's porch, a skinny and long, two-story house, packed in between other skinny and long, two-story houses with several others, all identical, surrounding them. It was early evening, dark and cold, with all the houses in the row lit, except for Mr. Hanlon's, number two-thirty-two, Slocum Street. John was collecting for the newspaper.

Mr. Hanlon's morning newspaper still lay on the porch and the television's light flickered on the kitchen wall and back door. John's breath steamed on the front door window as he looked through the glass. The wind banged the screen door up against his heel; the living room, dining room and staircase all completely dark. Dried brown and yellow leaves piled up in the corners on the porch. John knocked again and Mr. Hanlon never answered.

The next morning, still dark and cold, while John delivered the papers, stars lit the sky over the west mountain and began fading over the east mountain. Steam and smoke floated above the houses from the industrial park nearby. John lived in the Susquehanna Valley, and his route was his street, the next street, and the next street over. The street lamps were still lit and he could see his breath while walking in the middle of the street on the double yellow lines. Mr. Hanlon's flashing television the only light in any of the houses in the row; all dark and asleep. The wind blew up against the houses and the bare, silvery trees on the mountains.

John always walked in the middle of the road so he only had to walk up the street once, throwing papers to his left and right onto porches, side-arm, over-hand or under-hand. He quickly warmed up as he collected the bundles on the corner and put them in his bag. Folding papers as he walked, he fitted them with rubber bands in his coat pocket; never stopping, always walking while banding, stuffing or throwing.

Each morning created new challenges. Mondays the papers were the lightest, and often did not fly very well, and Sundays were the heaviest, requiring a perfect throw; decisions always being made.

For the entire week, stories and pictures about the Space Shuttle Challenger explosion filled the front pages; the seven astronauts; Krista McAuliffe, the school teacher from New Hampshire. John's teacher, Miss Coach, cried when she found out; cried in front of the whole sixth grade class. School let out early.

Both newspapers sat on the porch, the television still flickered in the kitchen, and John knocked on the door; looking through the window he waited for Mr. Hanlon to walk through the family room, wearing creased, polyester slacks, a button down shirt and the same beige, cardigan sweater. After the first knock he always appeared, every time, from behind the corner in the kitchen; walking slowly, he held bills and coins in his hand and would open the door. "Young man, come on in here," he would say.

John always stood in the family room by the door next to the cold radiator. He hated the burning kerosene smell in the house during winter; mothballs in summer; the stale, cigarette smoke smell in all the fabric and carpets year round. It was always so dark in there, too.

John knocked again, this time knowing that Mr. Hanlon would not appear from around the corner. The cold, front door knob turned easily. Quietly opening the door like a burglar, he stood in the family room and called out, "Mr. Hanlon. Are you home? Mr. Hanlon?" Inside the house, John's breath showed like steam from a kettle; the house only offered relief from the wind. He called out a few more times and Mr. Hanlon never appeared; the television in the kitchen the only sound in the house.

The feint kerosene smell along with a bad breath scent filled the house. John turned on the kitchen light, killing the television's flicker. Looking around the corner, he found a chair toppled over and Mr. Hanlon on the floor, curled up as if asleep on his side, facing John.

"Mr. Hanlon. Mr. Hanlon," John said, walking toward him, knowing he would not answer, but not knowing what else to say. This was the first dead body John ever saw and felt sad that his bald head rested on the cold, linoleum floor without a pillow. The color in Mr. Hanlon's face and hands was like a raw Thanksgiving turkey thawing out in the fridge. His face looked puffy and round, his wrinkles smooth, and fingers chubby.

On the kitchen table sat a box of Saltines, a half-eaten bowl of tomato soup, and the television; putting his fingers on the knob to turn it off, he looked down at Mr. Hanlon, his head on the floor, and decided to leave it on.

John thought to call his mother. Checking for a quarter to use the payphone on the corner, he saw Mr. Hanlon's phone on the wall, a yellow, rotary phone, bulky like a shoebox and stained from cigarette smoke. He looked around before putting the sticky handset to his ear; about to use a dead man's telephone. He heard the dial tone and called home. John's mother answered, and he told her about Mr. Hanlon.

"Okay, honey. Are you okay?"

"Yeah. I'm not hurt or anything."

"Sounds like Mr. Hanlon's had a heart attack."

"I guess. Looks like he hit his head on the floor."

"I know, honey," she said. "Okay, what's Mr. Hanlon's address?"

John told her the address without looking into his route book. He kept it neat, filled with names and addresses, and check marks. In the rows on the left, the names and addresses printed clearly, and at the top of the columns, the dates for each collection period; every two weeks. Whoever owed him money had a blank space in the box.

John walked through the family room to the front door, to go out on the porch and wait for his mother; with his hand on the door knob he looked back at Mr.

Hanlon lying on the floor, alone. He flicked on the porch light and a lamp in the family room.

A framed photograph on the wall showed Mr. Hanlon as a young man with his wife, wearing his dress blues. Another one on a mahogany plaque showed a young man, a soldier; an inscription read: Joseph Hanlon, Jr. Army—SGT—E5—1st Infantry Division. Oct 10, 1947—March 24, 1969. Palm Sunday palms were wedged behind both pictures at the corners. John gathered up the mail on the carpet and walked back to the kitchen and set it on the table.

He picked up the fallen chair and sat down; after looking at Mr. Hanlon, he looked away; pushed back the tomato soup; flipped through his route book and then watched the television, a small, eight-inch color set with the antennas wrapped in tin foil.

On the picture, hot air balloons floated over the countryside, all slow, big and colorful; drifting. It was autumn. All the deciduous trees were bright, the maples yellow and orange, the oaks fiery red. In the baskets, the pilots pulled cords and video cameras captured children smiling and laughing, pointing down to the farmland below, the brown and green patchwork of unequal, four-sided shapes rolling along the Appalachian foothills, and through the valleys.

The view focused in on one, purple and yellow balloon, flames shooting up inside and wind flapping into the microphone. The pilot, a bald, smiling man, alone in the basket, looked out at the countryside, and the towns and mountains in the distance. He wore goggles and a white jumpsuit like an astronaut.

John wondered if the Space Shuttle astronauts looked like Mr. Hanlon, calm and tired, chubby and white, and needing a shower. He was curious if the shuttle cockpit and the astronauts smelled like Mr. Hanlon's kitchen, if all dead people just lay there looking asleep. On the table he noticed Wednesday's paper with the explosion on the front page, a puffy mass of smoke with the blue, Florida sky in the background. The astronauts burned up in the fire, he realized, and that made them more dead than Mr. Hanlon.

John thought a little about the difference between Mr. Hanlon and the astronauts. Then he looked at the television and the view widened, the camera pulled back, and showed all the balloons again, floating through the sky in the same direction, like birds migrating, all drifting over the mountains in the blue daylight except for one balloon, the purple and yellow one with the solo pilot; and the picture then cut to a close-up of him looking directly into the camera and waving.

Breaking away from the fleet, he flew over the valley and all the towns, the small hillsides full of houses and churches, the buildings and factories along the river, on his way over the shadowed, north-face of a mountain filled with evergreen and touched with yellow, orange and red.

John's mother stood beside him in the living room while Mr. Hanlon was carried out on a stretcher, wrapped inside a black bag; her arm around him on his shoulder. "I'm very proud of you," she said.

"Why?"

"For taking care of Mr. Hanlon. Because he was all alone."

"Okay."

John's mother turned off the television and all the lights in the house. As they walked onto the front porch, John said, "I'll have to cancel his paper for him for tomorrow."

Confidence

Nancy used to have long, maple hair with loose curls that rested on her shoulders and fell to the middle of her back, which was smooth and gently curved like the stem of a calla lily.

Her Grandmother, Mom-Mom, was the only one who knew in those days that smoking cigarettes was bad for health, that it would wrinkle skin, take its life, its gentle curves, and dry them out to feel like worn leather or canvas.

Mom-Mom knew this because her Terrier, Butterscotch, would sneeze and leave the room when people lit up; sometimes even whimper and go downstairs, into the basement.

Nancy quit smoking the year she became District Manager of all the Dietitians in the Susquehanna Valley, but her hair has been short and manageable ever since her second child was two months, when enough was enough already of her one and a half year old's little fingers always tugging at her curls, often tangled and knotty from dried, chalky spit-up.

There were photos of Stephen around the house but only in family photographs, which had most importantly, the children in them—Dana, Steve and Greg. They were still a family, after all. Just because

Stephen found another lover, or lovers, did not mean they were not a family.

When Nancy was in night school, finishing her Masters, only several years after the divorce, she saw her friend Janet's photo album, which had Anthony, her ex-husband, cut out of every photo with a utility knife—the white, thin cardboard of the album his silhouette as if he were some kind of good-guy. The pictures showed his flat, faceless figure carving the turkey, swinging on the tire swing with their youngest, napping on the couch at Christmas while the kids tape recorded him snoring. Only an art teacher, like Janet, could cut him out so exactly, leaving the life of the photo in an attempt to kill his memory. Nancy thought about taking the family pictures down, but she realized that he was still their father.

When Nancy and Stephen were in college and dating, she hated kids, always afraid they would try to touch her, or ask her a question. For their three month anniversary, they went for dinner to a small, family owned Italian restaurant on the first floor of an old home. They stood in the foyer waiting to be seated by the hostess—a round, little woman with white hair tied up in a bun—on her nose rested reading glasses and another pair dangling around her neck.

A large family of many adults was seated in the back room. There must have been a dozen children running around the table, singing, laughing, and crying; screaming this, that, and everything else. Nancy took a deep breath. "Take me out of here," she said.

Stephen began pulling out her chair at a table for two near a fireplace. He told her not to be silly, that it would be perfect. A baby cried and a small child ran through the hallway.

Nancy turned around and walked out of the house, down the steps and out to the car. Stephen walked out to the car where Nancy was standing still, at her door, waiting for it to be opened.

"You can eat here if you want to, but I'm not going back in there."

The clouds blocked the sun up above Nancy while she sat outside on the patio at Harper's, a lakeside restaurant. The flat, afternoon light was soft and even across the water, in the trees, and in her dark, short hair touched with silver. She was there for a business lunch.

As a kid, Nancy and her sister went swimming at Harper's Lake, took hayrides in the fall, ice skating in the winter. Across the lake from the restaurant, the roller coaster frame still stands.

Nancy and Stephen had their first date at Harper's Grove, rode the roller coaster and danced to the band together all night.

Across the deck, there was a group of young people together, a table of eight, all laughing and drinking cocktails. The cigarettes were going and stories being told. There were only two young women, one beautiful, and the other was clearly involved with one of the young men; they sat close, fed each other food and kissed.

Thomas Schappert

Nancy knew that her youngest, Greg, was the same age as the table of young people and would fit in well with them. He was away at the State University. She wondered if he would try to gain the attention of the beautiful one, the way a few of the young men were. They looked through her and always spoke up above one another. The two that were closest sometimes touched her shoulder or back when she laughed at something they said. They sat up and pulled their chairs forward whenever she said anything at all, to anyone.

The beautiful one's confidence extended up above her straight spine and neck, outward from her square shoulders, and her back never touched the chair. Nancy noticed it never occurred to her to tilt her neck back and exhale cigarette smoke up above everyone's head.

Nancy smiled to herself at the thought of confidence, the highs and lows, its elusive nature, like the sun on a mostly cloudy afternoon.

Even after raising the kids, juggling babysitters, working, studying, going from one accomplishment to the next, one failure to another, all within the same week, day, or hour, for years on end, she wondered if she'd ever really known confidence.

The sun peeked out and was again covered up by the shifting clouds. Nancy looked out over the water to see the remnants of the roller coaster and the highlights through the clouds collapse back into the flat, atonal light.

Susquehanna Valley

The young waiter brought her coffee and smiled. She could feel the wrinkles at the corners of her eyes when she smiled back, the lines around her mouth beginning to form. Nancy saw the boats motoring over the lake and the children splashing in the shallow of the shore.

"How is everything?"

"Perfect, just perfect. Thank you."

"Can I get you anything else," he asked.

"No, all set, thank you. Well, a little more sun would be nice," Nancy said.

He smiled and said, "Yes ma'am. Sunshine. Coming right up."

Permanent

Will hit the remote, turning on the TV and pressing play on the wildlife video he rented from the public library. The narrator's steady, baritone voice spoke of African wildlife above hippos splashing and wallowing, elephants that sounded like a trumpet concerto, cheetah's chirping, porcupines rattling and vibrating their quills, stamping their feet and clicking their teeth.

Getting ready for the clambake, he dropped a tiny well of sunscreen on his palm, cool, with an unedible smell, and, after rubbing his hands together, he put it on his tattoos—beneath his t-shirt sleeves on his biceps and triceps all the way around both arms, down to his elbows. He soaked more into the front and back of his wrist and up the same forearm.

The phone rang and it was Ron.

"Not much, just watching a littlc TV, getting ready," Will said. He gave Ron directions over to the house. Ron said he'd be by in about a half an hour.

Will moved swiftly through the house. On his way into the kitchen to do the breakfast dishes, he kicked a shoe that his brother Pauly had forgotten about on the living room floor. Their parents left them the double block where they've lived all their lives.

Will made his way through the kitchen to the sink. The back door was open, letting in the warm breeze and the sound of the birds chirping—cars rolling through the alley; next door, a basketball bounced on the concrete. His sure hands worked steadily, soaping the plate, pan and utensils, rinsing and then putting them in the strainer at his side. He finished up, drying the dishes with a towel and placing them in the drawers and cupboards—juice glasses directly above, plates far to the right, bowls in between.

Leaving the kitchen, Will turned off the electric light above, smiling at its faint buzzing. Pauly left lights on, doors open and things lying around all the time.

Ron pulled up in his muscle car, louder than a jet airliner, and the Steve Miller Band pushed from the hot speakers. Will clipped his long-cane to a small caribbeaner attached to one of his belt loops. The cane was un-extended, and all pushed up like a compact umbrella not in use. Pauly once told him he looked like a Jedi Knight with a light saber dangling at his waist like that.

Walking down the old, front steps with an even, undisturbed pace, Will was met by Ron on the sidewalk. They shook hands. Ron said, "alright, man, let's roll!"

Steve Miller Band played and the car's motor idled with a loud gurgle. Ron opened his driver's side door. Will stepped onto the tree lawn and felt around on the car with his hand for the door handle. Before Ron stepped into the car, he ran around to Will, his feet pounding the pavement. "Oh, hey, I'm sorry, man," Ron said, "you need a hand?" Will had found the door handle by then and told him he was alright. Ron helped him close the door and said, "sorry about that."

The leather, bucket seats rumbled and squeaked with each move that Will made. He rolled the window down and fastened his seat belt, always facing forward. Vanilla scent filled the inside of the car and Ron's cigarette was strong, burning the inside of his nostrils.

Rolling through Will's neighborhood, they passed Stoney's Tattoo Shop where they had just met the day before. Will thanked Ron for inviting him and offering to pick him up. Ron told him more about the clambake on the ride. His friend Cutter throws it every year; calls it 'Cutter Fest.' There would be hundreds there, people from all over—bikers, guys from the plant, dart league, soft ball—everywhere. And all kinds of good food and beer.

"Whenever you're ready to go home, just let me know," Ron said.

"That's cool. But, my brother and his girlfriend said they'd come up for me."

"Either way," Ron said, "invite whoever you want."

The brakes locked up and the car skidded and screeched to a stop. Will rocked back and forth between the seat and safety belt, locking his legs into the floorboard and gripping the door handle, also the underside of the seat. Turning his head nervously, left to

Thomas Schappert

right, listening, he searched for sound, any indication as to what was going on.

The car rumbled in place. Smoke from burnt rubber on the pavement floated around the car. Ron turned off the stereo and took deep breaths, slow and loud.

"You alright?" Ron asked.

"What the hell was that?"

"Damn kids. That was lucky"

They motored out of town, onto a two lane state route in the country. Will felt the temperature drop a few degrees when he smelled Harper's creek and heard the falls on the side of the road. They drove past a dairy farm—manure and hay scents filled the air. Will took a deep breath and exhaled as if satisfied. Ron did the same but exhaled much more loudly.

"We heading out to 118?" Will asked.

"You bet. Then up onto North Mountain," Ron said.

Will's head slowly tilted and shifted, like a cat's ears, figuring. "We used to come sleigh riding out here when we were kids," Will said.

Ron looked over and smiled at Will who was attentive, staring straight ahead. He liked that he'd been sledding, and admired that he knew his way around, not only in his neighborhood, but outside of town, too. Will was his first blind friend. He was just trying to be cool.

———

Susquehanna Valley

They slowed down and turned onto a gravel road. The wheels crunched and crackled. The shade was cool from the trees hanging over; the dirt and the pine tree sap smelled moist. The sun flicked through the leaves on and off Will's arm. People talked while walking to the party, and they rolled slow past them. Car doors opened and slammed along both sides of the narrow road and there was a lot of laughter. As they neared Cutter's place, a garage band was playing "Smoke on the Water" and dirt bikes motored through the woods.

A pack of dogs ran out of the woods past the car as Ron cut the engine. They barked and bit at each other, their paws pounding the ground like a buffalo herd and scratching the gravel. "Here we are," Ron said.

Will opened the door, placed one foot on the ground and detached his long-cane from his side, which he held at chest level, overhand, like a chopstick. There was a little ball on the end that tapped on concrete and a strap that went around his wrist. He shut the door, took a deep breath of the country-pine air and followed Ron's voice, arcing the cane in front of him, side to side, hitting wheels, door panels and bumpers in the grassy front yard.

A quarter-stick exploded nearby and the thunderous sound echoed through the yard and forest, drowning out the band, the dogs, the birds, and Ron's voice.

Will banged his knee on the side of a car, caught himself on the hood with his hands and dropped his cane. He did not move until the reverberating echoes ended. The cane was at his feet, and he bent down to pick it up between two cars parked close together. Will said that he was ok, that Ron could lead him out of all the cars and bikes and he'd be fine. He grasped the back of Ron's right arm, thick and round, with his left hand and walked one step behind. Ron told him if that happened again he'd find whoever it was and punch their face. "No man, be easy," Will said, "it's all right."

They made their way to the cool and shady, back porch area. People were talking and the grills were hot and smoky, grease burning and sizzling. Ron knew just about everyone and introduced Will around. People reached their hands into icy water for bottles and cans. "Beer?" Ron asked.

"No, thanks. I'll take a Coke, or whatever."

Ron pulled out a soda for Will, and two cans of beer for himself. The sound of the dogs running through the woods disappeared as they reached the ridge-top and continued beyond. "You cool?" Ron asked.

"Yeah, I'm good. So, what is this place, Cutter's house, or a hunting cabin or something?"

"He lives here. We hunt here, too. Since we're kids."

"It's great out here. Out in the woods," Will said. "Is that a pond out back? Smells like a pond."

"You bet. Just out back a bit."

Little kids ran around playing in the grass, laughing and screaming. The band played "Wild Thing," the opening bars of "Stairway to Heaven" and "Smoke on the Water," again, before taking a break. Feedback screamed through the main speakers as the wind blew into the microphones.

"So, what do you do down the comic book shop?" Ron asked.

"I work the register mostly. Place orders, clean up and what-not."

"That's cool. Anyone ever rip you off?"

"Hardly ever. Couple times"

"You like comic books and shit?"

"Oh, yeah, my brother used to read them to me when we were kids. Describe the pictures, and the action, and stuff."

"Sounds like listening to a ball game on the radio," Ron said.

"Yeah, kind of, I guess," Will said.

"I like to listen to the ball game while I wash the car."

Ron smoked a cigarette and looked out into the yard. He saw Will facing the horseshoe pits, listening to them clank around.

"Did you ever play? Horseshoes?"

"No, never did," Will said.

Ron stood up. "Come on."

Will paced the length of the pit to get an idea of the distance between the stakes, his long-cane arcing side to side in the grass before him. Ron stood by, holding the horseshoes, seeming to try and protect him from something very particular, like long stares from people, or laughter.

"Can I see one?" Will asked.

Ron gave him one and he fit it in his hand between his fingers and thumb, swooping his arm back and forth, knees bent, practicing a toss. "Yeah? Just pitch it like this?"

"You bet."

Will's first few tosses fell short or over shot the stake. He paced the distance once more, and after that began to relax. His nerves were still a little tense, his adrenalin still running hot. The guys they were playing against had a game going earlier, and Ron did not like the idea of waiting until their game was done.

Ron had moved big and swift off the porch, through the grass, and over to the horseshoe pit. Will followed behind, listening to his booming voice. "Ok, we're up now," Ron said, moving in on their game.

"We're in the middle of a game here, man," the one guy said.

"Well, me and my buddy are ready to play now. He's never played before," Ron said.

"Yeah, but, we're in the middle of a game here," the guy repeated.

"I don't care what you're in the middle of. I'll put you in the middle of something-"

"Hey, hey, easy," Will said, "we'll play later, man. It's all right."

"Hey, listen. We'll play doubles. How's about doubles?" the other guy said.

"Yeah, doubles is cool. We'll play doubles," Will said.

"Alright then, doubles," Ron said. He exhaled loud and deliberate through his nostrils.

Stoney's Tattoo Shop was busy and smelled like the hair salon where Pauly's girlfriend worked as a stylist. People sat in the front room on couches, talking and looking through the binders of flash. Others crowded over the glass cases in the corner filled with studs for naval, ear, tongue and other piercings. High-speed, vibrating needles dispensed permanent ink into flesh in the individual studios down the hall from the waiting room.

Will's tattoo artist, Jay, was working on a fifty-year-old woman named Mary. Will and Pauly have been friends with Jay over twenty-five years. They've all seen a lot go down together. It was Mary's first tattoo, and she liked that Will was there. He was like an audience.

Jay's colorful hands, filled with tiny individual images he'd inked himself, were dulled through rubber gloves; one rested on Mary's hip for leverage. With the needle-gun in the other, he dipped back and forth from the ink into Mary's waist. His foot tapped the pedal, slow and even, powering the needle.

"My daughter thinks I'm crazy I'm getting a tattoo," Mary said.

"Did you ground her? I'd ground her," Jay joked.

"I can't ground her. We fight awful."

"Neither of you knows what the hell to do without the other," Jay said.

"Oh, I know it," Mary said.

"I don't know, kiddo."

An oscillating fan rustled the corners of Jay's drawings that hung on the walls. Most were images of animals, his specialty. A fish tank gurgled in the corner and college radio played on a small, clock radio in his personal studio, one of eight in the shop. Next door was a younger artist who specialized in body piercings. Punk rock pulsed through the painted waferboard that separated their studios. Will liked hanging around at Stoney's with all the different people and artists because it's a lot like Mega Comics where he'd been working full time, a few blocks down.

Will stood outside with Jay while he was taking a break, having a smoke. They were discussing Will's idea for his next piece. He wanted an eagle on the underside of his left forearm, whose wings stretched around to the top—the brown, copper, black and gold colors would blend into the bear and its dark, sunburst coat on the top of his arm. Jay smiled as Will pointed to images precisely—the bear's back, its head and neck, all its colors.

"Hey, man, let me see this. How's it looking?" Jay touched Will's arm on his sleeve.

"Feels pretty good," Will said. "How's it look?" Will pulled up his sleeve to show him the portrait of Jody, he and Pauly's dog from when they were kids, a fat-faced Chocolate Labrador.

"Looks good. All the swelling's gone," Jay said. "Everything cool?"

"Yeah, why?"

"You've been pretty steady from piece to piece for awhile now," Jay said.

"Yeah."

"I'd hate for you to play it out. You know what I mean?"

"I guess."

A nervous-looking guy wearing a suit walked past Will and Jay into the shop. He asked if there was a phone he could use to call Triple A because his car had just broken down. Ron was early for his appointment with Jay and was sitting in the waiting room looking at some pictures. He overheard the guy with his car problem. Will and Jay walked back into the shop to hear Ron offering him a hand with his car. "Let's have a look," Ron said.

Jay went to finish up with Mary and Will hung around, waiting for Pauly's girlfriend to pick him up. Ron and the guy came back into the shop so he could call off Triple A. He thanked Ron again and again for fixing his car. Ron said, "no problem," deep and loud.

Ron sat back down, next to Will, and he breathed heavily. When he spoke to Will his voice carried over the top of his head. "That's some beautiful work you've got, man," Ron said.

"Thanks, man."

"I like this little bumble bee right here."

"Thanks. That was my first one."

"That's cool. This is my first one." Ron pointed to a spot on the top of his forearm. "Oh, sorry man. It's an eagle with an American flag. I got it when I was in the service."

"Cool, man."

"Jay's going to touch it up. It's really faded. Few others, too."

Will was sitting at a picnic table on the front porch eating hamburgers in the shade. His back was against the edge of the table, and he faced the yard where the late afternoon sun was still hot and not too high above the ridge. A woman about Will's age walked by the front porch and smiled at him. "Hi," she said, walking up on the porch. He looked in her direction and said hi. She sat down next to him, facing out into the yard. She told him her name was Lena, and her elbow touched his while resting on the table behind.

"Do you know where there's a bathroom here?" Will asked.

"Yeah, right off the side porch, around back a little," she said.

"Thanks. Just around back? To the right or left?"

"It's just around back. Can I help you?" she asked.

"Sure, thanks."

Lena turned Will around to face the side porch steps and he held her arm. They walked about twenty yards behind the house on the cool, shaded grass from the trees above, her leather jacket rumbling and squeaking. When they reached the port-o-lets, Will said that he'd meet her back on the porch, that he'd be just fine.

The step up onto the porch was a pile of cinder blocks. Will's long-cane made a dull tap on them and then a sharp tap on the porch floorboards. Lena was sitting at the table, watching Will make his way back. When he sat down his knee touched hers and neither of them moved. They talked awhile. Her voice was direct and she enunciated words perfectly. Her leather jacket squeaked as she took it off. Sometimes her lips smacked up against each other as she began to speak. Will heard the differences in her voice when she looked at him and spoke, and when she looked out into the yard and spoke.

She told Will all about her motorcycle. He said it sounded cool.

"Want to see it?"

"Sure," Will said.

"I mean. Do you want to-?"

"Don't worry. I say *see* all the time. Like, 'Let's *watch* TV,' or, 'Can I *see* that?'"

She led Will around the house to the front yard, through the bikes and cars, his hand around the back of her arm, one step behind.

"Did you just get some work done here?"

"Yeah. A little bit ago. How can you tell?"

"All the dried out, dead skin."

He felt the leather seat, the cool chrome of the long, bent handlebars and their rubber grips. The bubble-shaped gas tank was rounded like a turtle's shell. Will asked what color it was, and Lena said orange. Will knelt on one knee to run his fingers through all the spokes, and along the tire tread. Lena held the bike still while Will sat on it, his hands up on the grips, his feet rested on the frame.

"Want to go for a ride?" Lena asked.

Thomas Schappert

"No. I don't think so. No thanks."

"Ah, come one. I'll take it easy on you," she said.

"No. That's alright," Will said, "it's ok."

"You ever been on one before?"

"Nope. That's ok. How about we take a walk out by the pond?"

They walked through the yard past all the kids and the band, toward the ridge. As they came upon the pond the ridge's shadow cooled the grass. The sun was on its way behind. Bottle Rockets whistled through the air and Roman Candles popped high in the sky—M80s continued to explode followed by cheers and laughter.

Lena and Will sat in the grass along the shore of the pond. Mosquitoes landed on their skin and buzzed by their ears. Perch and Sunny's made little splashes, swimming to the surface, feeding. On the other side, the teenagers were throwing large rocks into the shallow water, trying to splash one another with the lime-green, slippery water. The dogs came running down from the ridge and sped past them, barking and snapping at each other as they ran.

"How high is the ridge?" Will asked.

"Looks like a good walk. But not that high."

"Is there a trail?" Will asked.

The trail was a narrow dirt and gravel opening amongst the laurel and brush. Will held onto her arm and she led him up the trail, the way Pauly had done since they were kids. He asked that she tell him what she was seeing and to make him aware of loose rock

28

and big roots. Lena described the pines and maples on the mountain, the red rock and the shriveled, brown leaves left over from last fall. She called out 'left' or 'right' whenever the trail bent, and when she said 'roots,' Will stepped high and dropped his feet flat.

At the top of the ridge was a clearing where the sunlight broke through, facing west into the rippling, Appalachian mountains. It was warm and windy, blowing Lena's long, straight hair into her face. Will stood still, looking into the wind, listening.

The soft, golden sunlight warmed their skin, and it would soon be gone again. They sat on a rock covered with flaky lichen. They were high on the ridge, several hundred feet above the gully below. The Susquehanna Valley far in the distance toward the horizon, beyond the mountains.

Lena stood up to get closer to the edge. She yelled for Will to get up, to lean into the wind with her. She was held, suspended above the gully by its force. Her arms at her sides, her palms facing out, cupped, she was on her tippy toes, leaning, farther and farther into the wind. She cried out again and again for Will to try. "Come on, come on," she yelled.

"You're crazy."

She stood before him and poked him in the side a little. "Come on, give it a try."

"How do you know Cutter?" Will asked.

"Who?"

"Cutter. The party. This is his party."

"I don't. One of my biker friends, Ron, invited me. We ride together sometimes."

"Ron? Big Ron? Drives a Chevelle?" Will asked.

"Must be. Oh, yeah. You know him?"

The gusts continued to swoop up the windward side of the ridge into their faces and an eagle soared in its wake, riding the thermals high into the sky, way up above their heads. Its wings were expanded, curled, its light-brown underside exposed, and it leaned diagonally into the wind, facing the ridge, sailing up and out, away from the mountain over the gully in search of prey below. Silent the entire time, it was invisible. By the time it circled across the clearing, Lena caught her breath and exhaled sharply.

"Beautiful," she said.

"What?"

"Eagle."

"An eagle? Riding these thermals." Will nodded his head a few times.

She looked at him shaking her head slowly, smiling. "Yepper," she said. She told him all about it, and the eagle returned again and again; thermal winds lifting it high above the ridge to float over the clearing below. She held his hand and told him everything she saw—the eagle, the tiny, blue mountains in the distance, the even, bronze, shadow-less light of sunset and the countless shades of green.

"Do you wish you could see sometimes?" she asked.

"Not so much anymore. I used to."

"What's it like? I mean, what's the eagle look like to you?"

"It looks like, what it does. Its function. Like a bee, and how it stings. The first time I was ever stung is when I realized it. I felt it and, I saw it, in a weird way."

"Does that explain this?" She touched his arm.

"Yes, it was my first one."

Lena's thumb moved softly, unconsciously across the back of Will's hand. She told him how the eagle disappeared into the west, becoming a tiny black dot against the light-blue of dusk. They agreed they should get going down the ridge. Downhill is a little trickier for Will. He always stays directly behind Pauly, with his hands on his hips, to step where he steps.

Will put his hands on Lena's hips, soft and rounded, her waist slender, and on every step, Will's hands rocked up and down, and side to side a little. Lena shuffled down the trail quickly, laughing, her hands sometimes on Will's. She cried out "Let's go, let's go!" and Will's sure feet shuffled right behind.

The dark-silver light of dusk had set in on Cutter's yard. The teenagers were still hanging out by the pond, sitting in the grass, waiting for the fireworks to begin. Lightning bugs flashed throughout the yard. Crickets chirped underneath the bushes and in the woods. Colorful owl lanterns were strung up on the back porch and hung from tree branches throughout the front yard, side yard, and back to the port-o-lets.

Lena and Will walked through the yard and sat in the grass by the fire to wait for the fireworks to start. The kids were roasting marshmallows on sticks.

Their faces glowed. Some young, rowdy partiers came over to the fire with some fire-crackers and bottle rockets for a display of their own. They had beers and cigarettes, and they laughed and cursed while the kids clapped and sang songs with their parents. Ron walked by and saw those guys and what they were doing, his shadow big in the firelight and disappearing into the darkness.

"What the hell is going on here?" Ron asked.

One of the guys showed him their fireworks. He looked proud. Ron towered over them, blocking the light and heat of the fire. He threatened their lives with his fist.

"Take your shit out back by the pond with the other shit. There's kids around here. Somebody could get hurt."

Lena and Will heard the whole thing. Will smiled. "Good for him," Lena said.

"Yeah, Ron's a good guy to have on your side."

Ron saw them sitting in the grass. "Oh, you met Lena," he said, "that's cool." "Oh, yeah, and Jay is here."

"No shit?" Will said. "I can just ride back with him then."

The fireworks started; the crackles and booms in the sky followed the whistles and hollow-sounding thuds from being shot through lead pipes burrowed into the grass. Will held Lena's hand and she told him all the colors, the way they looked when they exploded, the way they seemed to expand from a single point, like the big bang theory or something.

"Were you ever able to see?" Lena asked.

"Yes. I went blind when I was about five or so. I remember lots of stuff."

"Like what?"

"Everyday stuff, like clouds and grass, trees and the sky. Our old dog, Jody. I remember my brother really good. And my house."

"That's good."

"It's pretty weird we saw the eagle. I've been planning on getting one right here," Will said.

"Yeah?"

"Yeah. I was all set on it, but now I don't know. I kind of feel like I usually do once it's done."

"It was beautiful," Lena said.

"It's always been the other way around."

Will tightened the chin strap. Lena tightened it a little more for him. "Here," she said. Will sat up on the bike, held up by the kickstand, leaning to the left a little. Lena fixed her own gear, her gloves, jacket and helmet.

Ron was also in the front yard, checking out his friend's bike, his voice loud and carrying through the dark air. Will got off the bike and called out to him. Ron was happy to see him, raising his voice and introducing him to his old friends. Will thanked him for the ride and everything and told him he'd be in touch soon, that he and his brother have a cookout at the house every Labor Day. Will said he'd remind him to invite Cutter, too. "Cool, man. Let me know when," Ron said.

"I'm going to get to work on a horseshoe pit."

"You should see this guy!" Ron said to his friends. "First time. A pro."

"We could have beaten those guys," Will said.

The bike fired up at the press of a button. Lena lit the headlamp. Will's feet were rested on the side pegs with his hands on her hips, but when she let out the clutch and pulled the throttle, his body jerked backward a bit so he wrapped his arms around her waist real tight instead.

An Arm's-Length Away

Being forgotten is probably the most inexcusable thing you can do. It doesn't take much to be remembered. You could keep quiet and be a hard worker, or you could smash your race-truck into a hundred-year-old oak tree and wake to find its picture in the newspaper. Either way, at least you're remembered for something. And, the fact is: remembering is living. All things worth living are remembered. Things happen, some worth remembering, and most were never worth living to begin with. No one I know sits around and tells stories about what could have, would have, or should have happened.

In the emergency room you can get a lot of thinking done while someone pulls glass from your face with tweezers for four hours. The smashed-up race-truck and the hundred-year-old oak tree are not bullshit.

One of the first things I remember is sitting in our living room with my father, eating bananas and watching cartoons. It was the day of the annual Giant's Despair Hill Climb. The first time I was ever there I was four or five years old. Earlier that day it was raining, the wind was blowing hard and the colored leaves were falling off the trees. The temperature was mild and the back door was open, letting in the sound of the rain and the wind, which rustled my drawings that were magnetized to the fridge.

My father and I were on the floor in front of the TV. Whenever something funny happened in the cartoon and I laughed, he tickled me underneath my ribs. When a loud gust of wind challenged the windows of our house everything except the sound on the TV stopped. He looked at me while the windows rattled. His eyebrows raised, suspicious, curious; his mouth open, appearing to be saying oh. After the wind died down, and it was nothing, he tickled me again.

We threw the banana peels all over the living room, and I ran from the kitchen, pretending to slip on them. My father had the blue, yellow and white Chiquita stickers on his face. He stuck them to my belly and all over the living room, on the TV, plants and furniture. He stood up on the sofa and put one on the painting, inside one of the yellow discs of the daisies; they were set in a fat, red vase and spilled up and out. In the background, the blue sky hid the blue in the Chiquita sticker; the white blended perfectly with the thin petals, the yellow with the discs of all the other daisies.

That storm was unforgettable, especially the clouds after the rain had stopped. I followed my father out onto the back patio. Red and yellow leaves lay all over the yard, piled up in the corners of our patio, and in the links of the neighbor's fence. We stood outside, barefoot, on the wet, smooth concrete. The wind up above the houses and treetops was ferocious because the clouds were moving fast, dark and gray, traveling east over the mountain. The storm had a definite beginning and end, and the blue sky glowed in the west. The line between the sky and clouds stretched from the horizon in the north to the south; it was directly above our house and then quickly moved east. It seemed it could have been raining in our yard but not in our neighbor's. All the while my father and I stood there and watched. By the time I finished my banana, the sun was out, the sky was blue, and the grey clouds were almost behind the mountain.

I stood there like my father with my hands on my hips, watching the sky. He said, "Looks like it's clearing up for the race. The road'll be dry in a little while."

Mom came home soon after to hear us laughing. She told us to clean up the banana peels and stickers, and to get ready for the race. I wore my brand new *Star Wars* t-shirt that day. I had just seen the movie in the theatre; it was the first one I ever saw.

The main reason I remembered that day, the strange line of clouds, their clear edge, the bananas, and that it was the day of my first Giant's Despair Hill Climb was because of Johnny Harmon, my friend Ricky's older brother. One day, in eighth grade, we were stranded at the middle school after detention. I don't remember why we had detention, but I remember our ride home.

We stood underneath the awning outside the front doors of the school. The November rain was painful and the wind loud. Darkness had been setting in earlier and earlier, but because of the storm it was already near dark. Standing up against the glass doors, we looked down the dark, empty hallway. That was the only time I remember wishing I could be inside the school. Because of the wind, we were getting soaked, and we were shivering. In the field on the side of the school the wind was blowing the rain in all directions, in layers, in diagonals and sometimes sideways. Every time I focused on the pattern it changed.

Johnny, a senior at the high school, sped through the parking lot in his pick-up truck to take us home. He plowed through puddles, made waves higher than the roof on each side. The truck was headed right at us; it looked cool. I was relieved because it was cold and I was wet. Ricky stood still. Standing still was a defense against the wind and cold for him.

Johnny pulled up in his jacked-up F-150. Standing next to it I could barely see over the hood. The truck was a dull black and looked creepy. Spots of peach colored Bondo were pasted all along the bed from the cab to the tailgate. The hood was primer grey, salvaged from a junkyard. On the doors, the phrase "Harmon's Moving" with a phone number was stenciled in faded, yellow spray paint. The truck's motor drowned out the metal on metal clank of the flagpole and the storm. He rolled down the window, a cigarette smoldering between his lips. "Get in needle-dicks!" he said, cackling and lifting his ball cap off of his head; while he was fixing it back on he ran his fingers behind his ears, tucking in his long, straight hair.

Susquehanna Valley

Ricky and I walked around the front of the truck and Johnny pulled forward a little, almost hitting us. He hit the horn and motioned with his thumb over his shoulder for us to get in the bed. We saw him over the hood, through the fast motion of the windshield wipers. He laughed and I looked out into the field, the wind and rain still dark and furious and blowing in every direction. Ricky shrugged his shoulders and said "figures," water dripping out of his thin hair.

The knobby tires were good for climbing into the back. We sat down on wet plywood and started pulling a tarp over us. Dirty water from inside the folds of the tarp spilled over us—cigarette butts and leaves part of the wet mix. I knew that I would be home soon because my house was only about five miles from the school, up on top of Giant's Despair Mountain.

Johnny looked at me through the rear-view mirror. Our eyes met and he boomed another big laugh. He floored the gas pedal, and Ricky and I were thrown into the back of the bed, which was full of junk tires, a ladder, a heavy duty jack and lots of other metal stuff that hurt. He turned left and right through the parking lot, and we were rocked in opposite directions, hitting the wheel wells and the walls of the bed. The tarp flew up from the wind. The rain stung our faces. We laughed out loud.

After a short drive out of the valley and a few turns up on the mountain, I knew that I was nearly home. Ricky and I were still laughing, trying to protect our faces from the wind and rain with the tarp. My road was just up ahead, but Johnny locked the brakes up and we were slammed up against the back of the cab. We looked out from under the tarp. Johnny had put the truck into reverse. He stopped short, cut the wheels sharp, and we headed up onto a dirt road. We used to ride bikes and play fort up there. We knew what was about to happen. We yelled, "Shit!"

Johnny had dropped the truck into four-wheel low. He took off up toward the mountain and the tarp was useless as we were wrestled around by the bumpy road. The truck roared through overgrown branches, splashing the puddles and climbing over logs that had fallen across the road. We bounced all around the bed, laughing, screaming and cursing.

Eventually we made our way out of the woods to the front of my house where I jumped out. I stood still, in awe. I looked at Ricky and waved, and I looked at Johnny and wished I could be like him. I heard his muffled laugh through the glass. He was laughing at me, standing in the rain, which had just slowed to a drizzle. I watched the truck disappear around the bend while the light from the late afternoon came back as the clouds thinned. I was soaked, my clothes, my book-bag, and the light rain seemed not even real compared to the storm.

By the time I walked around back the rain had stopped. I stood on the back patio, looking out into the sky. The edge of the storm was a long line of clouds, directly above my house; it stretched from the horizon in the north to the south. From the west, the light-blue sky was pushing the storm into the east over the mountain. I knew I had seen the same thing before. I took my muddy shoes and socks off and set them under the patio awning. Standing barefoot, I watched the storm go. The sun was low and dim when it appeared from behind the clouds. It soon fell behind the neighbor's house, pulling away from the storm.

I remembered then, with my bare feet on the cold, wet concrete when I'd seen that happen before. I remembered the sounds of the cars and trucks racing up the mountain, one at a time, to see who could get to the top the quickest, and running, pretending to slip on the banana peels in the living room; my father stood on the sofa, placed a sticker on the painting, and I laughed uncontrollably.

Shaking my head of dripping water I picked up my wet book-bag. The early evening was calm. The sky and the neighbor's house were reflected in a large puddle in our yard. I walked inside, through the kitchen and into the living room. Looking at the painting I stood up on the sofa the way my father had, when he pressed the sticker into the daisy's eye with his thumb.

It was still there, stuck on the painting, faded and crinkled. The blue, yellow and white were still hidden perfectly amongst the sky, petals and discs of all the daisies. I was amazed. After all those years. I wanted to be able to make people remember things.

I fantasized all the time about having a big truck like Johnny Harmon's. I knew that I would be famous, more famous than he was. I would take kids home, and just when they thought they were safe we would be four-wheeling up the mountain. My truck would be black, shiny black.

But mine would have light-blue flames on the side.

The summer between our freshman and sophomore year, Ricky and I worked every day at Mr. Kleen Car Wash. We washed, waxed and detailed cars and trucks. We even did Johnny's truck, which was cool. I also worked mowing lawns and doing odd jobs down in the valley. By the end of the summer I'd saved almost two thousand dollars. I was turning sixteen in October, and my dad was teaching me to drive a stick.

I bought my first pick-up truck from a guy named Carl Dicton on the other side of the mountain. Carl was short and stocky, barrel shaped. He had wild, curly black hair with lots of gray. His front yard was a fleet of trucks and cars, all in good shape. A Mustang was up on the lift in his garage with no tires or paint job and a smashed back-end.

In the spring, after all the trees flowered, the roads were covered with seed and slick little petals. The day I test drove the truck, the roads were wet and slippery. Carl watched me drive, and he watched the road at the same time. He stuttered with hesitation and pushed his foot into the floorboard around every bend. He was more afraid I was going to buy the truck than he was that I'd crash it.

Carl calmed down a little. We started talking and he asked me if my father's name was John Yavorski. I told him yeah, that's my dad. Carl smiled.

"We put the gym teacher's Chrysler inside the gym. There were about twelve of us; picked it up and rolled it right onto center court."

"Yeah, I've heard that story a million times," I said.

"Oh, yeah?"

"Yeah. And there's that other teacher. My dad ran his bike up the flagpole senior year."

"McKeowen? Must be him; rode his bike every-day," Carl said.

"You don't know about that one?" I asked.

"No."

"Gaiteri's still there. The gym teacher."

"No shit?"

After we drove around the country roads a little, he talked the truck down. He said, "It gets poor gas mileage. It's a gas guzzler. Terrible in snow, too." Carl's wife came out, pregnant, holding a baby. She was smiling that I was there, checking out the truck. He wiped away smudges on the chrome bumper with his flannel shirt. I thought about a lift system to get a few inches on it and some off-road, knobby tires.

I broke Carl's heart and paid him $1750 in cash right then and there. It took me nearly an hour to get out of there. He double checked all the fluids and told me what I should 'keep an eye on.' When I finally did begin to pull away, his hand was rested on the top of the hood; he kept constant contact with the truck, all along the side, to the back quarter panel, until his longest finger could no longer touch the tailgate.

"Tell your dad I said hi."

"Will do."

At the end of the drive, I peeled the tires out, kicking up gravel and dust. When I reached the road, the tires screeched and I fishtailed while he watched.

The crowd I ran with in high school was called The Stainers because we were troublemakers. We hung out at Levy Park, a small playground near the school with swings, sliding boards and a basketball court. We drank beer, chewed tobacco and talked about girls, cars, and fighting.

My first real accomplishment in those days was part of a Stainers initiation. We had to think of a prank, something risky, that no one had ever done. Johnny Harmon's prank was still talked about. He pulled it off when he was a freshman, way before the time he drove me and Ricky home in the rain. He was the only freshman ever let into the Stainers, probably because he should have been at least a sophomore, maybe a junior.

Mr. Gaiteri, the skinny, old gym teacher hated Johnny Harmon. He skipped gym all the time. And, when he did show up, he won at everything. Nobody could swim, bat, kick, run or anything better than Johnny. The baseball, wrestling, basketball and football coaches were always trying to get him to go out. Johnny told the Stainers he could put Gaiteri's Volkswagen Beetle inside the gymnasium, by himself.

Gaiteri and his class walked into the gymnasium one day to see his Beetle on center court. No one saw Johnny do it, but he set up long, metal running boards on the gymnasium stairs, put the Beetle in neutral, backed his truck up and pushed it up the ramp and inside.

I decided to call the cops on myself and say that there was someone vandalizing Levy Park. I said the vandal had a baseball bat. There was one light on a pole in the middle of the playground. The deal was that I would stand under the light until I saw one of the cop's feet touch the ground. I would not run until then.

The cops showed up, and I was their man, standing there under the streetlight with an aluminum baseball bat. They kept the lights on the cruiser going. When I saw the first shiny, black shoe touch the ground I took off. There was an auto parts store across the street from Levy Park, and a few of the seniors were up on top of it watching the whole thing.

I ran across the train tracks behind the playground into a small wooded area called Hobo Jungle. Homeless people lived there. I ran through the trees, and I could hear the police yelling. I could feel their flashlights pointed at me. I ran out of Hobo Jungle, hopped fences and ran through yards. My heart raced. I knew that I was making history, that I would never be forgotten. I ran through more yards and hopped more fences. I ran across the valley without stopping. There was a rundown dress factory across town with railroad tracks behind it. I walked over the tracks to the back of the building and sat down against one of the loading docks, behind a dumpster, breathing hard, listening. I had probably lost them a while back but kept running because of the adrenalin.

I sat there for a while in the dark, catching my breath and waiting. The rusty air became thick with humidity and a little chilly. Clouds covered the stars, and the wind dried the sweat on my head and back through my t-shirt. Leaves on trees and plants were all each turned over from the wind.

I looked around to see if anyone was coming. I looked down the length of the railroad bed into the darkness. Lightning flashed beyond the mountain. I started walking before the rain started. The railroad tracks went all the way back to Levy Park. I wanted to get back, to see the guys and make sure they saw me.

The wind was difficult to walk into and chilled my body. The rain came down hard and fast with no warning, no light drizzle first. I felt heavy drops on my head and arms before I heard its slap on the ground. I was soaked immediately. I walked fast, taking long strides and skipping railroad ties to get back to the guys. I figured they were waiting for me underneath the pavilion at the park.

I reached Hobo Jungle. I crept through the over-grown sumac and birch and got down on my hands and knees in the bushes, in the cold, wet mud. The vegeta-tion smell reminded me of playing fort and manhunt up on Giant's Despair when I was a kid. I looked into the lone streetlight in Levy Park to see the rain still falling. There was not a trace of life in the playground, no police, not even mosquitoes.

I would rather have seen the police with their swirling red and blue lights, making a spectacle, ques-tioning everyone. I would have rather been afraid, with my pounding heart from the thought of the police calling my parents. I walked into the playground to find the aluminum baseball bat still lying on the ground where I had dropped it, under the streetlight.

I walked across the street to the auto parts store. I looked up to the roof and whisper-shouted, "Guys! Guys!" But no one was there.

When I walked in the house, my father was on the recliner, his feet up, clicking through the channels. I sat down on the sofa and we watched *Honeymooners* and *M*A*S*H* re-runs.

I became a Stainer for my police chase stunt. I hung out with those guys all the time. We had black t-shirts with white lettering. On the front it said Stainers in all capital letters; on the back, our last name and a number. Some of the guys in sports like football, baseball or basketball had their jersey numbers; the wrestlers put their weight class. Seniors had black t-shirts but with red lettering.

We pulled lots of pranks just for fun. A warehouse down the street from Levy Park was its own city block. Trucks were always coming and going, all night long, off of the highway and into the valley. One thing we liked to do was sneak in there and get up close to the building to try and touch it. Someone once dared Johnny Harmon to do it during daylight. He said he would, and that's how it all started.

Johnny Harmon pulled it off no problem. He hopped the barbed wire fence and shifted through the sea of trailers and cabs parked in the lot. From the fence to the building was about three football field's length. Guys were always walking around, trucks coming and going. It was not easy to get up there without being seen, and touch the building. It also took patience. The seniors said that Johnny had to wait in between two trailers for a few hours. They said he came upon some guys working on a cab. There was no other way, they said. He had to wait it out.

One night, my friend and I hopped that fence and worked our way up to the warehouse. The sun was low on the horizon when we set out, about to fall behind the mountain. By the time we made it up to the warehouse, it was twilight. The flood lights were all lit on top of the building and on the poles throughout the lot. There were men all over, walking around, driving forklifts, carrying pallets; there were about fifty loading docks, and they ran the length of the warehouse.

For a few moments we sat at the wheels of a trailer that was parked in the first row, closest to the building. All we had to do was go about twenty five yards up to the docks, touch it, and then get back to the trailers. We walked toward the building. It was clear. My heart was pounding with adrenalin.

Because there were so many loading docks, it would never be perfectly clear. Johnny Harmon said that the only way to not get caught was to walk up to the building, and then walk back to the trailers, casually. We could only wait for it to be clear within the space of several docks on either side of us.

We walked up. We knew people saw us, but they were far away. We had to be confident that we were as small and unnoticeable as they were to us, that we were not suspicious at all. That was when I found out my old friend, Ricky, was working on those loading docks when we were in high school. We lost touch after he started up at the Vo-Tech.

As we neared the docks, Ricky walked out, lit a cigarette and looked down at us. He still had thin, blonde hair, but his shoulders and chest were rounded, his wrists thick. His head shook slightly and he smirked at the sight of us. He drew off of his cigarette and exhaled smoke. We stood still. He took another drag and gave me an up-nod. I gave him the same. He threw his lit cigarette on the pavement.

"Don't worry, man. I didn't see nothing," he said.

"Cool, man," I said.

He turned around and walked back inside. The building was only about 10 yards away, but we didn't move any closer. Even if it was only an arm's-length away, we wouldn't have touched it. It still wouldn't have been right.

"I didn't know Johnny Harmon had a brother," my friend said.

"Yeah."

"And he's our age?" he asked.

"Yes."

I pulled in to the lot at the bottom of Giant's Despair for registration into the race-truck class. It was a cool, autumn day; the oaks were bright red and the maples yellow and orange. I raced an '89 'Yota with a 305 that day; she looked beautiful, shiny black with my trademark light-blue flames on the sides. All my trucks, ever since the Chevy Carl Dicton sold me have been black with light-blue flames. I'd been working on it for months. I had painted an appropriate number twenty on each door because I had just turned twenty. On the tailgate and back quarter panels were decals advertising Tiny's Garage. I was working there doing body work. Tiny sponsored me for the race; he and all the other guys were there. My parents and girlfriend Tammy were there, too. I smiled to see Tammy's skinny legs jumping up and down when the announcer said, "Now racing, in number twenty, John Yavorski."

Muscle cars and race-trucks were everywhere, people lined up and down the mountain on the sides of the road. They stood behind plastic orange fences and bails of hay. It was just under a quarter of a mile from the start at the bottom to the finish. People were not allowed on certain turns because they were too dangerous.

The most famous of all the turns was a 135 degree switchback called Devil's Elbow; the whole run depended on that turn. After the Elbow, a short, steep incline reached 28 degrees. No one in the race-truck class ever took Devil's Elbow faster than fifty-five miles per hour.

I took the Elbow at sixty-three. I locked my wheel to the right, down shifted into second and pulled my handbrake. The back end slid out through the turn. I turned the wheel to the outside and floored it. My RPM's were redlined up the incline, and at the top, I shifted into third. There were a few more turns that I screamed and hollered through. The last stretch up the mountain to the finish was a fifty-five yard straightaway, steeper than the one out of the El-bow. I began in third, and with twenty-five yards left I downshifted into second. The finish at the top of the mountain peaked and then flattened out. At the top, just past the finish line, the lots on each side were full: one with racecars and race-trucks, the other with sou-venir and concession stands. Both lots were full of peo-ple and on either side of the finish line they crowded around. Trees lined the side of the road and the perim-eters of both lots.

I motored across the finish line with the fastest time; five seconds ahead of the leader. I locked the wheel up again to the inside, pulled the handbrake and slid the back end of the truck out almost hitting the souvenir and concession stands. A cloud of dust kicked up, which made my truck invisible for a few seconds. I pulled the brake again, maxing the wheel to the out-side and revved up the RPM's all the way. Letting the brake out, I started doing doughnuts, my back end always touching one of the lots on either side of the road. Dust kicked up into the judges' booth, conces-sion stands and all over the other racecars and trucks. The kids loved it.

I circled around and around several times, squealing the tires, losing control of the back end in the gravel. When I pulled the brake to stop, I slid and broadsided a hundred year old oak tree. My driver's side front quarter panel and door were smashed. The glass shattered and got into my face, arms and chest.

There was a lot of blood—it didn't look good. Tammy freaked out when she saw me. The impact also broke one of my shin bones and dislocated my shoulder. I was stuck up against the tree, unable to open my door. I looked through the passenger's side window to see people running toward me.

The medics pulled me from the wreck. I was hobbling on my one good leg; somebody had me around the waist. Who knew that Johnny Harmon had been to night school at the community college for E.M.T. training? He was grinning, shaking his head. They set me down, beside the ambulance. Johnny was dressed in blue with a stethoscope around his neck and a CB clipped to his belt squelched. He gave me the drill. How many fingers was he holding up? What was my name? Where were we? "That was some nice driving out there, John," he said.

"Thanks."

"You fucked up pretty good, though. They're going to disqualify you."

"Yeah, probably. But they know what time to beat."

"I guess. But it don't matter until next year," he said.

"What do you mean?"

Johnny worked for a few minutes, checking my reflexes, shining a light into my eyes, putting stuff into his kit, taking other stuff out. I looked around at the people looking at me.

Johnny broke the silence. "Hey, listen, I picked up an old Willys. Needs some body work, a nice paint job. I haven't been able to get to it."

"Yeah, just come down the shop," I said.

As I was being helped into the ambulance, I smiled to see photographers from the newspaper snapping shots of my truck all smashed up against the tree; people were crowded around, watching the tow-truck hook up to the bumper. Men with orange vests that said STAFF on the back were sweeping up the broken glass out of the lot. I heard people talking about my time, the fastest time, and the doughnuts. But I also heard another race-truck racing up the hill, its RPMs red-lined, its driver downshifting, its tires screeching, and other people cheering it on.

Bank-Barn

Curtis Nelson bought Harry Meyers's farm out on 520 the previous spring. The barn had not seen an hour's worth of work in over twenty-five years. Beyond the meadow behind the barn, Harper's Creek flowed at the foothill of the mountain, cold with run-off water, and full of native trout. When Curtis told me about the farm, the first thing he mentioned was the trout stream, perfect for fly fishing, filled with wild brook trout and that he had been fishing it since he was a kid.

The barn, an old Pennsylvania Dutch style bank-barn, was built into a small hillside, creating two ground-level entrances—the upper, right off 520, and the lower, facing south out into the meadow. All the animals were stabled below, and the fodder, wheat and straw up above—then lowered through the granary. To me, the whole set-up was amazing.

The first job was cleaning out the barn. One step on the floorboards released enough dust to make you cough, and after a day's work of hauling out old timber and scrap metal, the snot in your rag was hard and black, like little pieces of gravel.

One thing about working with Curtis was that he was always right there alongside you, especially during the worst jobs. I wore a hanky around my face, over my nose and mouth, like a bank robber, but Curtis never did. He said that all the dust and dirt kept him healthy. Every day he wore a gray pocket T-shirt, blue jeans, his leather work boots, and his silver, wire rimmed glasses. One truly amazing thing about him was his gray hair; it never moved, always nice and neat and parted on the side, no matter what job we were on.

The hay mow was once packed tight and neat with bundles that could be pitched below, wrapped in hemp string; Curtis said he wanted to clean the entire thing out. The dried out hay bundles fell apart with one easy tug. He hired a local waste removal company to bring out a dumpster—thirty square yards, and that's where we put it all. I figured we could easily fit about four Volkswagen Beetles in there.

Curtis said "the thing to do" was pitchfork the straw into a wheelie and then walk it on a plank into the dumpster, but when it became too full, we had to close the door and then pitch the stuff over the side. That slowed things down. Underneath the straw in the hay mow there was a lot of garbage like old *Playboy* magazines from the early 70s, old cans of Budweiser before ring tabs and dozens of empty, glass gallon jugs of apple-jack. We filled three of those dumpsters in the first week, just the two of us, mostly with scrap metal and wood, cardboard, hay, straw, and old chicken feeders.

Folks who lived out on 520, and nearby, would stop by to say hi and meet Curtis, curious about what was going on. They liked to walk around, out in the meadow and inside the barn. The smell in there was very compelling, the straw and fodder, the cedar—all reminders of the past. Everyone agreed it was a shame about Harry Meyers and what happened to the farm; he'd been sick for many years and no one in the family was interested in keeping the place up. His kids sold it soon after his death.

One lady who stopped by said that Harry told her she could have two huge rolls of barbed wire. Curtis told her sorry because he was planning to use it for fencing out in the meadow. Another guy came with his business card—a painter and scrap metal collector. We had just finished filling a load full of junk he could sell, and he said he'd come by a few days later. When he did he made a mess. Curtis was pissed. Another guy came by who used to work with the horses for Harry back in the 70s. He used to take kids out horseback riding on weekends. There were trails all over those hills and meadows along the creek, and in the groves. He wanted to get that started again. Curtis was interested, but the guy basically wanted to stable all his horses for free. Curtis threw his card away as soon as he left.

Mrs. Bortz, who lived next door, came by one morning in the rain. She was old and tiny, walking slowly and holding an umbrella. Her eyes were moist and curious. "I'm a hundred and eight years old," she said. And then she asked me my name.

"Andy," I said.

"No. Not that. Your family name."

"Oh, Haddaway."

"I don't know any of them," she said.

"Well, I'm new to this area."

"I see."

Curtis came over and introduced himself, and she said, "I know. I know who you are." I thought it was funny because she spoke to him like he was a child. They talked for over half an hour, about Harry Meyers, the barn, the farm, and all the old days, when Meyers' farm was the biggest farm in the entire Susquehanna Valley region.

There were forty-five acres of land once worked full time. Harry Meyers had cows and goats, horses and chickens. He provided meat, fowl and dairy products for almost the entire valley at one time, and employed many people. All year long, milk was sold out of the storeroom. People brought back the glass, wide-mouthed jugs and took away cold ones filled with milk. They also sold eggs and produce—pumpkins, tomatoes, cucumber, apples and blueberries. The *Susquehanna Voice* was on sale along with tobacco products and candy.

There were always people around, people stopping by; in the summer, they were there until late, when crickets chirped loud and fireflies flashed. Saturdays were for horseback riding and there were always kids around playing ball, fishing and picking blueberries; in the fall there were hayrides and apple cider; sledding in the winter.

The old Meyers farmhouse stood on the hill above the barn. Moss filled the cracks in the foundation. Mold grew all over the transite siding up to the second story where sun had been unable to hit. Two, huge pine trees in the front yard blocked any view of the house from the road. All around the house, forsythia, juniper and lilac bushes had grown into and up the walls. Shutters hung slanted from a single nail. Squirrels went in and out freely of basement and attic windows; mice, too. Dozens and dozens of honeybees swarmed the southeast corner. No one had done one day's worth of maintenance on the house in twenty-five years, except for the former tenant, Bob Thatchfield.

A few years ago, Bob nailed a four by eight piece of plywood onto the kitchen floor after he stepped through the linoleum and scraped his leg on a floor joist.

I was the first one to meet Bob Thatchfield. It was a Saturday, late in summer, warm, and the sun set a little earlier every evening. I was working on cleaning out the hay mow myself, picking up a few extra hours. Bob had white bushy hair, long and wavy, a white beard, thick and round. His rectangular glasses were silver, the lenses thick and tinted dark. There was a guitar on his holey T-shirt from some folk festival he'd been to in the early 80s. Frays on his cut-off jeans were loose and hung down. His sporty sandals with Velcro straps were not suitable for rummaging around the back of the barn.

We walked back there and he showed me what he wanted saved: a kayak with duct tape spots all over the bow, a dresser and a recliner. The rest we could throw out. I told him I'd tell Curtis.

Bob told me how he had lived in the farmhouse for twenty-five years and how he had just moved out one month ago. He still came by, everyday, to feed the hummingbirds and the barn cats. He and his wife were still attached to the old place and did not want to leave; it was where they had fallen in love and spent their whole lives together. I empathized with him about that. He was holding pruning shears to take clippings of all the forsythia, lilac and rose bushes around the house.

"You guys are really starting to clean this place up," he said.

"Oh, yeah. Curtis does not play around," I said.

"What's he planning to do with the place?"

"Not too sure. Pretty sure he wants to get some horses in here."

"Oh, great. What about the house? What's he want to do with the house?"

"Oh, that'll be coming down after a while, I'm sure."

"Oh, no. Really?"

Bob pushed up his glasses and looked out, up at the old house. I could tell the thought of it pruned away at his identity, clipping memories and feelings like branches from an old tree.

"I've spent my whole life here. Came here when I was a kid. Lived here."

"It must have been nice out here in those days," I said.

He didn't say anything to that. He just exhaled deeply, looked around and said, "Summer's almost gone."

Bob said he'd be back in a few weeks for the kayak and the other stuff. I told Curtis about everything and he said he needed to talk to Bob, that he was "a real wingnut."

I never could figure out how he lived in that house so long. The mice were so bad that they couldn't keep food in anything but plastic tubs. The honeybees had taken over the back bedroom; they kept the door shut with an old towel shoved in the crack between the floor and the door. "The bees don't bother us, and we don't bother them," he said. He told me about the plywood on the kitchen floor, that it "just became normal after a while." I told him I knew what he meant because I kind of did. I used to drive an 86 VW Jetta with door handles that never worked right and, like Bob, I'd gotten used to them myself.

The hay mow was finally cleared out and swept up; the granary, too. We completely demolished a loft in the back of the barn that was constructed out of birch tree trunks. Curtis drove the tractor in there and we hooked chains to where the posts met the beams, and we took it down in one day. But first, we had to move Bob's stuff to the front of the barn. Curtis had called Bob two days earlier and told him that he had two days to get his stuff out, or it was all going on our load.

Bob came by to get his stuff just after we took the loft down. We had disrupted a couple yellow-jacket nests and were both stung a few times. I stuck a pitchfork right into one while trying to clear out some straw.

Thomas Schappert

They were still swarming around in the back and Bob wanted to go back there to see what we'd done. "Stay away from there," Curtis said, "they're very aggressive."

"Look at them," I said.

"What? The bees?"

Bob walked back there in his sandals and stood still looking at the new view of the back of the barn; the yellow jackets swarming all around him.

Curtis shook his head and left to get some spray to douse the hives. We were done back there for the day.

Bob finished loading up his stuff into his Subaru wagon and looked around. He was surprised at how much more we had done with the barn and asked a lot of questions. We talked about the place and as he looked around, he started blinking quickly and pushed up his glasses, putting his hands in his pockets and taking them out, putting them in, and taking them out. He never looked at me when I talked to him.

Other than working out at the farm, the job I liked best was the Crayon House, a two-story home in a residential neighborhood down in the valley. The brick-face on the first story was a sandy, light-yellow color with maroon mortar, and the second story was cedar shakes. A young couple bought the house in the 70s, turned it into a day care and named it the Crayon House.

They put up a fence from the alley in the back to the front sidewalk all the way through the yard. The boards were two by sixes with the tops cut to rounded tips, like crayons, and they were painted red, yellow, green, orange and blue successively down the line. Everyone in the neighborhood knew about the Crayon House because of the fence. I lived around the corner from there during college and used the fence as a landmark all the time.

We renovated the house inside and out. The place was a mess, nowhere near as bad as Bob Thatchfield's little farm house, but it had been neglected for a long time. After we finished the inside, hanging drywall throughout the downstairs, replacing windows, countertops and appliances, sanding and re-finishing all the hardwood, tiling the kitchen and bathrooms and painting all the walls and ceilings, we started outside.

All the cedar shakes needed to be re-stained with a sealer and the rainspouts replaced. The front steps were cracked and a lot of brick in two of the front porch pillars were loose. We re-poured cement for the front walks, applied mortar to the loose brick and re-painted the front porch floor boards and all the trim around the windows and doors. There was nothing Curtis could not save.

After we landscaped the entire front and back of the property with new plants and shrubs, placed river stone all around the foundation and pruned the trees, the crayon fence was next. Curtis was planning to rent the home to a family, or young professionals, so the fence was unnecessary. We went at it with our pry-bars, cat's-claws, and hammers, and the fence was soon on its way to the city dump.

Thomas Schappert

The neighbor asked about the crayon fence; she was concerned about the fence, asking why we were taking it down and what was going on. I thought it was funny that she had not one word to say about how nice the property looked after all we'd done. She did not care. Several other people asked us about the fence, too.

A few blocks down from Public Square, the Hotel Sterling, built in the 1890s, became run-down and was abandoned in the 70s. It stood nine stories high and was once the most beautiful building in town. The marble lobby was lit with huge, crystal chandeliers. Inside, there was an elegant, five-star restaurant. For twenty-five years the windows were covered with plywood and loose brick crumbled onto the sidewalk. But everyone was sad when the building was razed and not just because Frank Sinatra had eaten there, or FDR had stayed there.

The Crayon House was once filled with kids inside and out, running around and laughing. Even though the house was quiet for over twenty years and became a wreck, people were sad to see the fence go; like the building, it just became part of their lives.

Mrs. Bortz liked to sit on her porch and watch us work because every day we started and completed projects, either big or small; they were all like little battles that we won.

One day, early in the fall, when the tips of the birch leaves were just beginning to yellow, we were working outside the barn and along the road with the tractor, clearing out the dead brush and trees, pulling out the rusted, iron fence posts and picking up trash. Folks driving by beeped and waved to us, smiling. Curtis liked that.

Bob Thatchfield drove by that morning like he did every morning, on his way to the VA Hospital, where he worked on the mental health floor. He had moved down the road a few miles to another old farmhouse. Sometimes I'd see him coming in his Subaru wagon, and if he saw us, he waved, but he never really looked at us. He just wanted to see what we were doing, noticing every tree we trimmed or stone we moved.

By early afternoon, Curtis was on a ladder fifty feet up in the two pine trees in front of the house with a chainsaw. He clipped the tree bottoms even with the upstairs windows, bringing light to the house, and making it more visible from the road. The tree limb pile was about fifteen feet high in the air and about twenty feet wide. And, we had the other pile from the dead brush and trees that was about the same size. I was pitching the limbs up on top one by one after a while because the bucket on the tractor could not reach.

The barn looked naked without the overgrown and dead sumac all over the walls. We spent a few hours inside, cleaning out the bottom. Some shelving and casing for chicken feeders were rotted and needed to be pulled out. There was a lot of cardboard and scrap wood around, and we placed it at the bottom of the brush piles, using it to get the fires started.

Curtis came across a dead groundhog in the corner underneath some junk he was pulling out. The little guy was about twenty-five pounds and furry. He had to have very recently crawled in there to die because he did not smell at all. Curtis did not want anything to do with him.

I left him there and worked in that corner, and once we had the piles burning hot, I scooped him up with a flat head shovel and pitched him in.

The last time I saw Bob Thatchfield was the day we painted the barn late that fall. It had never been painted since it was built. The cedar planks, once a vibrant red, one hundred twenty years later, by the time we got to them, were weathered down to a dull, orange-rose.

Curtis figured we would paint the barn red, to "really spiff it up."

We met out there at dawn, and it was soon a beautiful, fall day. There was not a cloud in the sky, the sunshine was mild and colorful leaves filled the trees. Curtis had two of his friends come out to help with spraying the barn, and between the four of us, we had three spray guns.

Ladders were all over the side of the barn—forty, twenty-five, and fifteen foot extension ladders along with step ladders from ten to four feet; it was like an assembly line, guys coming down one, going up another, finishing sections at a time while Curtis and I moved them forward, always making them ready. He engineered the entire project and it was brilliant. I was the cut-in man, with a cut-bucket and four-inch brush, trimming out the sides of the barn, the bottom on the stone foundation and around the windows for the spray guns.

I learned to love being thirty-five feet in the air on an aluminum extension ladder, swaying and bowing in the wind from my shifting weight, painting a cornice, or some eaves. Curtis had set the ladder up. And that was all I needed to know because it wasn't going anywhere.

I used to work as a hotel front desk clerk, standing in the same place every day, watching the cars go by outside, feeling like I was missing out on the world, wearing dry-clean-only clothes, and it smelled the same in there every day. At the end of the day there was no feeling of looking at what had been done, like when I looked up and saw the barn, as red as the leaves on the oak trees in the season's peak.

The compressors for the spray guns drowned out the birdsong, the horses in the field across the road, and the wind in the trees, but I smelled the manure, the dead leaves, and of course, paint. We double-coated the barn that day, covering over fifty-five hundred square feet. Looking at the barn in the end was barely proof because it was so unbelievable.

We were finishing up the second coat on the last side of the barn, late in the afternoon, when I heard three cars honking their horns. I turned to see them behind Bob in his Subaru wagon, driving five miles per hour, staring through the passenger side window at the new, red barn.

Thomas Schappert

I knew the view Bob came upon that day because I had seen it earlier that afternoon. Curtis sent me to the Contractor's Warehouse for four more five gallon buckets of paint, and on my way back, when I drove up over the hill and saw the red barn, I was thrilled. It was a beautiful sight.

The sky was blue, the trees were mixed with green, yellow, red and orange, and the big, red, bank-barn stood like it had always been there, like a monument, a monument to the land and the people who worked it, and loved it.

Curtis and I used to crack jokes about Bob all the time—the honeybees, the rats and mice, the plywood kitchen floor, that he probably had humming birds nesting in his beard, let his cats eat with him, put their food and water bowls on the table and pushed in their chairs. But we never made any more cracks about him after that day because Bob had a heart attack early that evening and almost died later that night.

The next morning, Curtis and I were up on ladders with cut buckets and three-inch brushes painting the trim around the barn doors and windows—a nice, soft-yellow. It looked "really sharp."

Mrs. Bortz came over with some banana bread and told us about Bob. Curtis looked me in the eye, and it was the first time I'd ever seen him look confused. He knew that he and Bob were about the same age, and this really threw him. Mrs. Bortz talked a little about the old days, when Meyers' farm was "really something." She said she remembered Curtis and Bob, when they were little kids. "Really?" Curtis asked.

"Oh, yes," Mrs. Bortz said. She laughed about how Curtis always wanted to help the guys fixing things and how Bob cried when the chickens were killed. She told Curtis how proud she was of us for fixing the place up so nice, that it looked "beauty-full," and that she was glad he bought the farm, and not "one of those other jokers." She said she was going to make Bob and his wife a chicken-pot pie.

After we painted the barn, we worked on other jobs downtown at some of Curtis's rental properties for a few days. The guy who wanted to stable his horses for free called back. He and Curtis reached an agreement because the next time I was out at the barn, there were about eight horses out in the meadow and a few in the stables. We were working on securing the fence around the meadow and heard sirens.

An ambulance stopped in front of Mrs. Bortz's house, and the EMT's took her out on a stretcher. She was already dead. Her daughter found her sitting in her late husband's recliner with an afghan covering her legs; the radio set on NPR and her breakfast dishes still dirty in the sink.

Curtis told me I could go out to the farm to walk around or fish anytime I wanted. Late that fall my girlfriend, Jessica, and I went out there in the afternoon. It was very late in the fall but sunny and mild. All the trees were bare except for a few oak trees, with their brown, shriveled leaves still holding on.

Jessica knew all about the work I'd done because I talked to her about it all the time; at dinner she would move food around unnecessarily with her fork; in the car she would switch the CD, or thumb through a magazine. Learning about how to fix things and maintain properties was new to me and was not so much a part of what brought us together. We met in college where I studied history, and she studied psychology. We had books, movies and music, stuff like that in common.

I was so excited for Jessica to see the farm. I showed her the inside of the barn, the hay mow and where the yellow jackets were nested. We walked out to the house and saw where Bob's honeybees had swarmed around the window. She knew all about Bob Thatchfield, and Mrs. Bortz. "Was she really one hundred and eight years old?" she asked. I told her that's what she said. I showed her Curtis's trout stream and the meadow. Of course, he was out there that day, riding in the tractor, giving the fields one last mowing before winter. She mostly wanted to look at the horses and shoot pictures of them.

Jessica did not care about all the dead trees and overgrown brush that once smothered the barn or its weathered, cedar planks. I should not have expected her to care about the barn like me, but I did. I thought I could express everything I had done and felt by showing her. But instead I started feeling ripped off. I felt like a visitor in a place that I identified with. I hated, all of a sudden, that other people were enjoying what my hard work had helped to create. Jessica understood this, but my sadness grew because there was nothing I could do except deal with it. She was right.

Susquehanna Valley

When we got back to our apartment, I looked around at the water-stained walls and ceilings, the scuffed linoleum in the kitchen, the shredded carpet at the top of the stairs from the previous tenant's cats, the dirty, cracked Venetian blinds in all the windows and the dozens of boxes filled with books in the spare bedroom.

The spare bedroom was supposedly our office, and there was only a small foot path through the junk to the one, operating computer. Our desks were cluttered with boxes piled up to the ceiling, blocking the windows.

I called our landlord and told her everything I'd need—about four gallons of paint, nine inch rollers, covers and pans, two brushes, forty square feet of floating floor to cover the linoleum, thirty square feet of carpet and padding for the hallway, and all new blinds. She was excited about it and asked me if I could do all of this. "Not all this weekend," I said, "but yes, I can."

The carpet in the office was an eggshell-white, in pretty good shape so I did not mess with it, except for steam cleaning. After I got off the phone with the landlady, I went down to the home improvement store. I fronted a couple gallons of paint and supplies to get started. We decided on a warm, candy-apple red for the walls and antique-white for the ceiling.

The trim around the door and windows was a wood-finished, lightly stained cedar. I picked up ten, twelve foot long, two by eight planks for the bookshelves, and five two by fours, all cedar. I found some polyurethane that matched the stain on the trim perfectly.

By the end of the weekend, I had two coats of paint on the walls and ceiling, the lumber sanded and stained, and the bookshelves completely installed.

I made the entire wall adjacent to the bathroom, one, giant bookshelf. I varied the spacing between the rows here and there, for big books and little books. Jessica used the space well, placing photographs and plants and things amongst the books.

On my desk, she placed a photograph of a large, brown Stock Horse standing by the fence with the bank-barn, the silo, and the blue sky in the background.

Last Call

I've got as many regrets as anyone, really—should have gone into the closet with Claudia Schaffer at Josh Tyler's birthday party in sixth grade even though I knew Carl Mancini liked her first, bought the Honda Accord, a more reliable, economic car instead of the Firebird in high school, or, more recently, talked to the girl at the bar who smiled at me and touched her hair. But I just turned with the round of drinks and went back to my friends at the table where we were studying for finals.

One of my biggest regrets, is that I did not accept the beer that my grandfather, Pop-Pop, offered me while he was terribly sick just before his death.

Pop-Pop had prostate cancer, which became a monster, giving him one standing eight count after another, backing him into the corner and up against the ropes, knocking him down round after round. He was always tall and able—broad shouldered with an appetite and a pot belly that hung over his belt. I used to love watching him play with Sandy, his German shepherd. She growled and chewed on his fist in the family room during the Notre Dame games. He always drank his beer from a pilsner glass, the bottle right beside on the end table.

Thomas Schappert

My brother, Paul, and I went to see Pop-Pop when we found out that he was in the final rounds and could not fight much longer; the chemo wore him down, took too much out of him.

Our grandmother opened the door and let us in. The front room did not get afternoon sunlight and was dark. "Boys, I'm so happy you could come," she said. "Your grandfather is so glad to see you."

"Oh, John," she said, as we kissed hello, pressing our cheeks together; her thin, painted lips were dry. She smelled like a department store. I couldn't believe how little she had changed; still with her short, curly blonde hair-piece and dark, penciled eyebrows. She kissed and hugged Paul, smiling at us, our youth and strength. We offered hope and good health to the house, that Pop-Pop would soon get better.

The house looked the same, and smelled familiar. I realized it smelled a little like my father's house and that it was likely to be the way my own house would smell one day.

Outside, the sky was clear and a cool breeze swayed the trees. The sun was warm, but not too hot. I was ashamed of my thoughts, thinking of what a nice day it was and all the other things I could have been doing.

The white, upright piano was still in the front room, clean and in perfect tune, as if someone played it every day. Through the 50s and 60s, Pop-Pop was the best piano player in the Susquehanna Valley. He played the big band, Tommy Dorsey style Saturday night swing, the ballroom, quick-step and slow-step

Friday night foxtrots, waltzes, tangos and salsas, high stepping at the keyboard, sweating, locked in with the drums and bass, commanding the trumpets and trombones. He was fucking good.

At Christmas time, I used to sit on one side of him, the low end, with Paul in the treble while he played on the white piano. We liked "Walking in a Winter Wonderland," the way he sounded like a concert hall full of one thousand instruments, loud, with his fingers spread wide from pinky to thumb, keeping bass lines and dropping chords. His treble hand even busier, arcing up and down, back and forth, keeping rhythm, harmonizing, and making melody all at once. His posture was perfect, and the force of his upper body seemed to push us onto the floor while the musical inertia pulled us back in, like meteors into Jupiter. It snowed every Christmas at Pop-Pop's.

I never will be sure if it snowed every time—as a kid, kneeling on the couch, looking out into the woods through the family room windows, making sure it was still snowing, white on every bare limb and clumped in the evergreen branches. Although it may have only happened once, its memory, and anticipation, made it real on each visit.

All throughout the house, the relics were clean and in their place, and though the family room seemed smaller, the furniture had not changed, nor moved. The carpet still carried a faint dog smell. Outside the French windows, bird feeders still hung; the only thing that did change was the forest Sandy once ran through, having been clear cut for a split-level home, Easter Sunday-yellow with green trim.

Pop-Pop lay on his side on the couch, using all his energy to keep his head up. An egg-shell white afghan stretched over his chest down to his knees, covering up the colostomy, trying to cover his fatigue, and shame. His delicate, feminine looking hands were hairless. His fingers were skinny and white. All the liver spots had disappeared from the tops of his hands. His bass-hand fingers tugged slowly at the afghan, fixing it, moving it, making sure. Sometimes he flattened out wrinkles with his palms, working up and down his legs and across his belly. He apologized a few times, silently, for being tired. We were all seeing each other together for the last time, and outside, it was a beautiful, Indian-Summer day.

One of Pop-Pop's more lucid moments was when he offered us a drink, which, I imagined, was the last drink he ever offered to anyone.

"Have a beer? Helen, bring the guys a beer, please?"

He died soon after, on a day that looked like summer, sunny, the trees green, chrysanthemums in bloom and the grass thick and high. But the wind was autumnal—and though it was nice in the sun, the shade was chilly. He was buried in St. Christopher's cemetery after a short prayer service in the chapel with only a few family members and close friends.

The autumn had come and gone, Christmas, winter. Second semester, finals, and graduation.

Susquehanna Valley

Late in the spring, my family arranged a mass for Pop-Pop at St. Christopher's. My four aunts and five uncles all came from around the country with their families. My uncle Emil spoke about Pop-Pop, his sense of humor, his selflessness, and compassion. He told a story about how he used to play piano for all the soldiers he served with in Europe, men who missed their families, their homes, their lives. Pop-Pop brought home to them for a little while in the evenings—songs they knew from childhood, from high school dances, the radio, movies, the songs of home. He spoke about how he still continues to bring us together, that he will always be with us.

Days later I drove back to school, where my friends and I were packing our apartments up and moving out, some for jobs to New York, D.C., or Chicago—others to Grad School—some staying in town with no idea where to go, or what to do.

After a full day of packing and cleaning, and an entire evening of drinking, the bartender yelled "last call," and one of my friends ordered two more pitchers for the four of us. Ben Folds music played on the jukebox. Our pilsner glasses were filled and we held them up to one another above the bar, all touching, our tone serious like during a eulogy, as if the beer drinking determined our friendships, our future.

"To making money. And I'm talking about making *a lot of fucking* money."

"To Lizzy Hetzel. And the *best* fucking blow job I ever had."

Thomas Schappert

"To Lizzy Hetzel. And the best fucking blow job *I've ever had*."

Everyone laughed, and I looked through my glass, at its familiar, curved shape; after the last toast was made and everyone began to drink, I raised up my glass a little bit more and said to myself, *"and to Pop-Pop."*

Varsity Jackets

James walks into Murphy's with his girlfriend Cindy, but the guy behind them holds the door for her.

Cindy hugs an old friend from high school by the dartboards and talks for a few minutes; James finishes a drink while holding up a bill, trying to get another.

Cigarette smoke hovers overhead, and heat pushes into the bar room from the fryers, ovens and grills in the kitchen; Hendrix "Fire" explodes into the Happy Hour air from the jukebox. Murphy's gets pretty crowded on Saturday evenings.

Scott Cole sits at the bar, his arm loosely on the back of his wife's chair; Murph places their drinks in front of them and then they begin to chat a little.

James drinks Red Bull and vodkas one after the next, all the while standing directly behind Scott and Jillian; he raises his voice while talking to another young man. He raises his voice talking to people across the bar. He raises his voice talking at the television, and while ordering drinks with Murph.

The Steelers and the Browns are all tied up in the third quarter of an AFC playoff game. Fans are bundled to protect from the cold and snow, their breath frosts and hovers over the stadium like smoke in a bar room. Some fans are shirtless, with painted heads, screaming and drinking beer.

Thomas Schappert

Scott catches college games on Saturday and the Steelers whenever he can; loves a good game. His arm is still on Jillian's chair, and he leans in, talking with her as James continues drinking and raising his voice.

A few months back, in October, a couple of young guys got rowdy, causing a ruckus in the back room; some still wearing their varsity jackets. A pool game got out of hand back there and some of those young men started raising their voices, throwing pool cues, trying to take each other down; Murph and some of the guys walked them out and told them to go home. But they just went around the corner to Sveboda's and behaved the same way in there. The cops took a report and Billy told them all their names, but nothing ever happened. Sue was behind the bar that night, and she put a round for everyone on one of the young men's card; but even that left everybody still a little thirsty.

Jillian's ring is a re-worked antique, discreet and elegant. She wears a sandy-cream, v-neck cashmere sweater with a light-blue, silk oxford underneath; the top two buttons are unbuttoned, and around her neck is a silver necklace with a clear crystal. Her dark blue jeans have a slight, boot cut to fit around her black, square heeled leather boots.

Scott usually wears work jeans, an old button-down shirt, boots, and a cap when he comes into Murph's after work, or on the weekends. Tonight, he and Jillian are out for dinner and drinks, and he wears new jeans, his good boots and a nice, tucked in corduroy shirt. In a couple years the corduroy shirt will move into a work shirt; still in good shape but so weathered on the neck line from his beard—even after his evening shave.

James's varsity jacket is the same maroon with gold trim as everyone else's; competing weight on the sleeve; senior year record on the left breast—24-0; and a bulldog on the back. Of course for football, numbers sewn into the sleeve and starting position on the left breast. The sleeves at the wrists and elbows and around the collar of James's jacket look like someone rubbed fresh printed newspaper all over them.

On a big third and one, all action behind the bar is stopped. Murph leans into Scotty and Jillian's space with a dishrag on his shoulder, like he and Scotty are back in the huddle together. Murph says that Coach would have nine in the box; Scotty grins and nods his head once. After the play, James begins yelling at the television, using obscene language directly behind them.

A rush of cold air opens up by the dartboards and jukebox as a group of young men enter. They are all wearing their varsity jackets. Murph looks at them closely while putting some money into the register. They spot James and make a lot of noise, shaking his hand, and shadow boxing him; one of them puts James into a chicken wing. They all call him Pulaski.

James jokes that they're not much bigger than when they came into the gym as eighth graders a couple times to work out with Coach Cavuto. They're surprised he remembers that. James tells them he remembers everything from senior year.

Jillian's chair gets bumped a few times in all their excitement; Scott keeps his arm on the back of her chair and never looks anywhere but at her, or the TV.

James continues with the foul language, and Jillian turns around. Murph takes a good long look at James; with his hands in the air, at shoulder level, he brings them down slowly to his belt and rests them a second, then, puts them back up and brings them down again, like a quarterback trying to silence a home crowd.

, James blinks a few times and shows Murph an up-nod; he then puts a ten down, finishes the rest of his drink and pushes the glass to the edge of the bar.

Murph picks up his glass, but with his other hand raises it up, though not as high as before, and brings it down a little, though not as low as before. James blinks and squints.

Jillian talks to Murph and Scott about how back in the day, Smitty wouldn't have had that kind of talk around here in the evening like this; no warnings.

Scotty holds his jaw and smiles, shaking his head quickly a few times; he tells Jillian that she's right. Murph looks away into the past, at the wall, and he smiles as well.

Jillian says she teaches these kinds of kids; she goes on about 504 plans and how these kids think they can do whatever they want, without any consequence.

Lenny walks in with his girlfriend; he's been working with Scott for about five years now; does all the drywall. As they walk in, Scotty slowly up-nods to Murph and pushes some bills forward. Murph then puts a drink chip in front of them both, and before beginning their drinks, they thank Scott. Scott just lifts his mug up a little bit toward them before having a little.

Another big play. The Steelers lose the ball on a fumble mid-way through the third quarter. The young men in varsity jackets all raise their voices in disgust, but James shouts foul language and kicks the empty bar chair next to Jillian, and Scott is on his feet facing him now.

Murph is downstairs changing a barrel of beer. Scott tells James that there are ladies here and that the language and volume are not necessary. James blinks his eyes a few times and his shoulder twitches; he tells Scott that he didn't mean to kick the chair, and that it is just a chair anyway. He asks Scott what the big deal is.

Scott says it's not about the bar chair; he's not going to have anyone talking like that in front of his lady, or any other lady, and that the rough-housing is not necessary; he reminds him that he's already been warned. Scott asks for an apology, and James smiles, looking around; he asks Scott if he is serious, all the while smiling. Scott just stands there.

Murph comes upstairs to see Scott and James face to face at the far end of the bar. They're about the same height, though Scott may have an inch or so on him. But James is almost twice as wide; his rounded shoulders and barreled torso shadow Scott's lean frame. Murph is standing right there on the other side of the bar.

Thomas Schappert

The varsity jackets are crowded behind James Pulaski; Lenny takes his cap off of his head and quickly puts it back on, and he then gets up from his bar stool and stands at the jukebox with one eye on the whole thing.

Scott tells James that there was a time when he wouldn't have gotten any warnings. And James wants to know what will happen to him if he doesn't stop. Scott tells him that at the very least he'll get thrown out of here on his belly. James wants to know what is the very worst; he then pats Scott's shoulder with his open hand three times, each time a little harder than before.

Scott takes a long, slow, deep breath, and he looks into James's eyes. Jillian stands up and tells Scott that it's not worth it and asks him to sit back down; let Murph handle this.

But James will not let it go. He steps closer to Scott and provokes him with his silence and his presence. Scott reminds him that he has not yet apologized.

Murph asks James to leave, telling him he's had too much to drink by now, and that drink a little bit ago was his last anyway.

James tells Murph whatever; he then looks to Scott and lets him know that if he still wants the apology he'll be waiting outside to tell him. Scott tells James he's going to finish his beer and watch some more of the game; he then tells him that if he's still outside after that, well, then that's his business.

After James and the other varsity jackets leave, Lenny comes over and tells Scott that he's got this;

says that he doesn't need to get mixed up in this kind of shit. Scotty nods his head, understanding, and tells him it's alright.

Jillian finishes her drink and stands up to put her coat on; burrowing her hands underneath her hair at her neck, she pushes them up to let her hair fall loosely off her shoulders and back, onto the outside of her coat.

Scott finishes his beer and stands up. Murph, from behind the bar, picks his hands up in the air and lowers them real slow. Scott nods his head and tells Murph that he's just going to sit him down, that's all.

Jillian walks to the ladies' room, and Scott tells her that he'll be waiting outside for her. Scott walks out the back door and Murph picks up the phone.

Outside, James is still out there and all the young men are standing around; their hands in their jacket pockets, jumping in place as if getting ready for a match.

Scott tells Pulaski about how this doesn't have to happen, that he could still apologize; the back door cracks open and Lenny walks out on the little deck, standing in the shadow.

James tells Scott that he doesn't apologize to anyone for anything, and Scott tells him that he is an embarrassment to them all, wearing that jacket and acting like that. He reminds him that he was not coached like this.

James shoves him and says that's all over now; ancient history; then asks him what he's going to do about it.

Scott puts his hands up to protect himself and James hits him with a left-right combination and then again with another right; all square in the face. The three punches put Scott off-balance by a half-step. Stepping with his front foot, and at the same time, planting his back foot into the ground like a goal post, he throws a right-cross that hits Pulaski square in the mouth and knocks him back into the maroon and gold sideline.

The back door opens and as Jillian walks out, Lenny goes back inside and takes his seat at the bar.

Some of the young men are kneeling down at James's side; they slap his face and encourage him to get up, saying it's not over yet. Pulaski just lies there on his belly. They stand still, staring at Scott with wide eyes and long faces.

Scott takes Jillian's hand and apologizes to her; she says good for'em, but no more of this, ever again. They disappear into the shadows of the parking lot; Jillian's heel's clicking and crunching on the gravel and concrete.

Inside, Murph sees the ambulance lights through the front windows. A police car directly behind. He walks outside and tells the paramedics that this young man had a little too much to drink, and on his way out, he fell down the stairs and cracked his face off the pail of sand and cigarette butts.

James Pulaski comes around instantly from the smelling salts. Everyone listens to Murph tell the whole story to Officer MacGrady, he and Scotty's inside linebacker. All the young men watch with wide eyes and mouths shut; MacGrady talks out of the side of his mouth a little bit about how it's still the third quarter and there's a pretty big crowd to watch a guy smack his face off a pail.

Murph kneels down by James and says next time he won't have quite so much to drink; then he pats his shoulder three times, each time harder than the last and asks, isn't that right Pulaski?

Right-Side Up

The infant cries. It cries, and it cries long and hard until it is exhausted and sleeps.

Cigarette butts, ashes, and dead match sticks almost fill a cereal bowl crusted black with spaghetti sauce on the coffee table in the front room. Amongst fast food bags, wrappers and cups, beer bottles, empty cigarette packages and the remote control, a neat little pile of toe nails and fingernails sit next to the ash-bowl in front of the flickering television; they are gaunt, and yellowed, as if they too are stained with cigarette smoke—like the plaster ceiling, paneled walls, make-shift curtains, furniture, and carpet.

The infant is about three months old, and if it isn't feeding or asleep, it's crying. It cries so loud and hard, he turns up the volume on the television nearly all the way to drown it out.

The cigarette smoke warms the living room. Six pairs of crusty tube socks lay under the coffee table. The beer bottle between his legs no longer sweats; David Letterman laughs. The infant screams.

He's been drinking whiskey and beer for the past two hours, waiting for her to come home with the oxy's, hoping that she gets home soon with the oxy's. The screen door opens on the front porch, the key goes in the lock and the storm door opens. A rush of

Thomas Schappert

arctic air fills the room and rustles the bedspread that hangs over the front room window.

She nods her head, sits down on the couch and takes out a pill bottle, all before taking off her hooded sweatshirt and jacket.

Colleen pushes the cart through the grocery market, through all the people with their carts and baskets. Following the cart in the maze of aisles, she holds on, walking slowly behind. Wearing a black overcoat, black business suit, a white oxford, and black heels, she continues forward, eyes open wide and not blinking; her complexion pale and heart rate low, and even. This is her third time down this aisle.

All the food in the aisles is secure in the packages and containers, the wrappers and cans, bags, jars, and cellophane, and Styrofoam; all needing to be decided about and then opened, combined, prepared, eaten, and cleaned up after.

Frozen vegetables cannot be eaten frozen and will remain frozen. Fresh produce never gets washed under cold water; instead it becomes soft and wrinkled.

Quickly reaching for a can of black beans off of the shelf and then, standing still, she hangs the can over the cart in her hand like a bad memory. Tortillas and cheese are back in dairy; tomatoes and onion in produce need to be cleaned and chopped. Leftovers need to be packed in Tupperware and used later. She faces the can back onto the shelf.

Colleen holds the cart with her fists, clenching the bar and supporting the grip with her knees, her legs, and the remaining strength in her arms and shoulders. Standing there, gripping the cart, she begins sobbing. Soon, tears flood her face, makeup runs onto her lips; her face hot. She sobs and sniffles, trying to catch her breath.

She pushes the cart down the aisle, through the open check-out lane, onto the automatic door mat, and out the door. A high school kid takes the cart from her. She says thank you and walks out into the parking lot to her car.

Inside the car, she sobs, staring straight ahead, her nose running with mucous; she calls her boyfriend, Greg, and tells him where she is.

He drives right over, parks next to her and reaches over to open the door.

Colleen steps onto the front step, a single piece of crumbling, concrete block. She sees the mailbox hanging on by one screw. The screen door does not close entirely, letting in insects, bugs and spiders. Black mold grows in the rotted trim around the storm door and window, along with the banisters, spindles and railing. Dirt kicked up from the street covers a Big Wheel on the front porch with cracked handlebars.

Ricky answers the front door. He smiles wide and stands on his toes when he sees Colleen. He shakes his bangs from his eyes. Taking her hand as she walks through the front door, he shows her a city that he is making out of junk drawer stuff and other things around the house.

Colleen cannot step much further than a few feet inside the door because magazines lay out in rows, covering the entire floor in the front room. In the center of the floor, amongst the magazines, sits a Monopoly board, tilted on a diagonal like a diamond. The magazines are spaced a few inches apart on all sides, like a grid; Ricky explains that these make up the city blocks, and the Monopoly board is Public Square, where they put all the Christmas lights. All the carpet spaces between the magazines and Monopoly board are the streets. He has Matchbox cars placed at intersections and all around town.

Two separate rows of couch cushions, pillows and clumped up blankets, parallel to one another, run the length of the room containing the magazines and the Monopoly board; these are the mountains, he explains.

Blue strips of cut construction paper a few inches wide run the length of the town amongst the magazines, parallel to the couch cushions, pillows and blankets; these make up the Susquehanna River.

An ashtray on the cover of a *Redbook* a few blocks south of Public Square is Ricky's house; a block to the east, a coaster on another issue, is where he goes to school.

On the Monopoly board stands a copper-plated metal bank, a replica of the actual Public Square Bank. Colleen remembers these piggy-banks were issued years ago to those who opened new checking accounts. Surrounding the bank on the board are other junk drawer items acting as the buildings and businesses on Public Square—a deck of cards, a spool of thread, a book of matches, an eyeglass repair kit.

Colleen tells Ricky that the city is wonderful, but she has to go talk to his mother. He squeezes her hand tighter and shows her a city inside the city, a big patch of carpet at the end of the town, along the river. He explains that the carpeted patch is all grass and trees. He has emptied all the pennies in the Public Square Bank out onto the carpeted patch. Kneeling down, he picks up handfuls of pennies with his hands, lets them sift through his fingers and fall to the carpet, saying that these are the kids, and this is where the kids live and play together; just them, just the kids. Colleen asks about animals, if they can come too.

"Oh, yes. Dogs and birds and horses are all there, too."

Greg rolls over, and opens the window to hear a lawnmower next door; the warm breeze comes in the room. Three cats laze at the foot of the bed in sunspots. Outside, patches of puffy, white clouds drift past; the trees filled with soft, lime-green leaves.

Colleen rolls over, tugging the covers over her shoulders; she keeps her eyes closed and asks Greg to shut the window.

Greg tries to convince her to get up, and get ready, so they can get out on the bikes. He sits up, stretches, and tells her he'd like to cruise up North Mountain, maybe take a walk on the Fall's Trail and get some fresh air, then ride down the backside, around Harper's Lake, and get some lunch—sit out on the deck looking out at the water.

He tells her that he'll get the bikes filled up while she's getting ready.

Colleen is on her stomach now. Burying her face in the pillow, she says, "No. I don't think so."

Colleen smells the cigarette smoke from the kitchen as she swats a fruit fly from her face.

Ricky talks more about the kids' city inside the city. He squeezes her hand as she begins to walk through the dining room into the kitchen, but she continues, telling him she'll be right back.

Colleen walks into the kitchen to see Ms. Selinski sitting at the table. She wears a bathrobe, her hair oily and falling onto her shoulders in clumps; her cigarette smolders in the ashtray. On the table, Colleen sees some Vicodin, Percocet and a plastic bottle of vodka with about a mouthful left. Ms. Selinski slumps forward, her chin at her chest, hands in her lap; she leans slightly to the left with her eyes half open.

"Ms. Selinski. Hello, Ms. Selinski. Ms. Selinski"

Walking back into the front room, she takes Ricky's hand and says that they're going for a ride now. Ricky looks up at her to see her eyes all puffy and red, her lips quivering; tears falling from her eyes. He asks her why she's crying, and she says that she is sad. Ricky walks her to the door and opens it. Colleen tells him that they're going to her favorite diner for some lunch and then for an ice cream. After that, she explains that she wants him to meet a super nice lady named Tracy that will look after him for the day where he can play outside with the other kids.

One of Colleen's seven cats is a cancer patient who must be fed with a syringe twice a day. She must take the formula and zap it in the microwave a few seconds to warm it a little.

She picks up Reuben, using both hands on her belly, talking in a high-pitched voice. She puts her on the dryer. Before she puts her thumb and forefinger into her mouth and spreads them to insert the syringe, she pets her for at least fifteen minutes. She rubs her head, her face, her butt and belly. She even rubs her paws a while, sticking her fingers inside them and stretching out all her little kitty toes and kitty fingers.

Colleen sticks her fingers into Reuben's mouth but only when Reuben is ready. She puts her thumb at the roof of her mouth and her forefinger on the bottom row of her teeth, but Reuben will lick them and nibble them a little bit first.

Colleen gently injects the syringe into Reuben's mouth. She talks to her the entire time, in a calm, soft voice. She calls her "little monkey" and "mama."

She's not home; won't be back until late. He has to stay there with the infant; it cries all day. It cries loud, and it screams. He closes the door to its room, and it still cries.

The blue bedspread hanging in the window pictures white lighthouses with red spirals; the tops lit up with yellow. The lighthouses are arranged graphically in rows right-side up and rows up-side down.

The lighthouses are draped over the curtain rod; they allow only a sliver of light from the outside to come in onto the ceiling.

He sits on the couch, with his elbows on his knees, leaning over the coffee table. He is crushing some oxy's underneath a ripped-out magazine page with the back of a spoon. He crushes them down into a fine powder and uses a business card to make a few lines. He then takes the straw from a soft drink cup filled with melted ice and the backwash of an unfinished soda. He rips off a two inch length of straw with his front teeth and sticks the rough end into his left nostril.

The lighthouses fall down and the sunlight shines in like a wake-up call. He has to get up, and hang it back over the curtain rod.

At the coffee table, in the dark, he snorts the oxy's, one line into each nostril.

The lighthouses fall again, letting in the sunlight, sudden and bright. He gets up, bunches the lighthouses around the cone-shaped trim at the end of the rod and ties each end off with a tube sock.

He walks into the kitchen and pours a glass a few fingers high of whiskey, drops in some ice cubes and rattles them around a few times. He opens his throat and pours the whiskey down. Crunching ice with his incisors, he prepares the baby formula and pours himself another drink.

When the baby formula is ready, he fills the bottle and tops it off with a few splashes of whiskey; he downs his drink and walks to the infant's room with the bottle in hand, chewing ice.

Colleen pets Reuben in the kitchen. Greg comes out of the bedroom with his shirt tucked in and wearing cologne. He opens up his cell phone to see that they're running over twenty minutes late. He reminds Colleen. She tells him that it will just be a few more minutes; Reuben is almost done eating. Greg exhales through his nostrils and says, "Of course, just a few more minutes." He then comments on how he told Billy and Amy that they'd be there by now. And, that he told Colleen two hours ago that they were meeting them by six.

Colleen apologizes as she kisses Reuben on top of the head; she is almost ready. Greg talks about how it's been the same thing for a year or more; if it's not some kid from work, it's the cats, or some neighbor kid who's hungry and needs a grilled cheese; he says that she is not their mother.

Greg picks up his phone, wallet, and keys off the table; he is leaving to meet Billy and Amy; he's already late. If she wants to come, she knows where they'll be; says he hopes to see her there. The screen door shuts behind him.

Colleen buries her face into Reuben's belly and fills her fingers with Reuben's fur.

Thomas Schappert

Stephen, Colleen's supervisor, sits at his desk. Light fills the back of the office through the window behind the desk; on the painted drywall hangs a few framed professional degrees and certificates, and there are some posters tacked up that show nature images. Colleen walks into the office.

Colleen's face is red and she holds a thick, file folder with both hands. She immediately begins detailing this woman's credit history, job history, police records, income tax records, and her file at the DMV.

Unfolding his hands, Stephen takes off his glasses; she continues about her deficient accounts with the electric company, water and gas companies, phone and cable companies and various companies who have sent the accounts to collection. Stephen gestures, opening his hands and says that all of this is excellent work, and well done, but he would like to know which case she is talking about.

"Ms. Selinski. Anita Selinski. Don't you remember? Ricky? Remember? I told you all about this little boy." She flips through the file with her head down. She looks up at him, waiting.

"Yes. I remember"

"Good." Her voice cracking, her pace increased, she then continues with statements from the neighbors and the landlord, rehabilitation centers, previous employers, Ricky's school teachers and multiple private childcare professionals.

Stephen nods. He tells Colleen that he'll get the process rolling right away. She looks him in the eye, says thank you, runs her fingers through her bangs and

98

lets them fall; she wipes her eyes and her nose with her fingertips and then turns to walk out.

The high ceilings and the marble floor in the Susquehanna County Courthouse lobby bounce the sounds of people's heels, voices, and doors opening and closing throughout the hallways. Small sky-lights high above let in some light and show the blue sky.

Ricky and Colleen sit on a wooden bench outside the door to the courtroom. Ricky wears a t-shirt, jeans, and sneakers. She wears a black business suit, white oxford, and black heels; she crosses one leg over the other, and her arm rests on the back of the bench around Ricky. She leans in toward him, working her fingernails over her knee, making wrinkles through the fabric in her pants, and then smoothing them out with the tops of her fingers by flipping her hand around and pushing it forward. Ricky sits still with his hands in his lap, scissor-kicking his legs up, out, and under the bench.

A painting of the Susquehanna Valley hangs on the wall directly in front of them above another bench; it shows the mountains of the valley, and the plains on each side of the river lush with oak trees, long before Europeans settled. In the foreground, an Iroquois sits on horseback, facing the valley below.

Ricky asks Colleen questions about the elevator. He explains that he's seen them on television. She asks him if he'd like to ride it to the top floor. His face becomes wide with excitement, and he gets up to walk over toward the elevator. She takes his hand and asks him to sit down.

She asks him if he knows why he is there, at the courthouse. He says that his mom has to be there and so does he. Colleen tells him that's good; it is because of his mom. She tells him about how his mom's sick; she's not well and cannot take care of herself right now, nor can she take care of him. She tells him that his mom is going to go live in a place where sick people live so they can try and get better. She continues with how he will live with a nice man and woman, and they will be his foster mom and dad; he will live there, and they will be his mom and dad and take care of him.

Ricky says that he wants his new mom to be Colleen, or even Tracy, because those kids were nice and she had hamsters. Colleen promises that she will talk to him on the phone and come over to see him. He asks about his mom, when she will get better so they can go home. Colleen tells him she doesn't know, and that she might not get better, that not all sick people get better; some sick people stay sick for a very, very long time.

Ricky begins scissor-kicking his legs quicker than before. He hears the bell for the elevator and turns his head quickly in that direction; he then quickly turns to Colleen.

Colleen drives in her state-issue car, a four door Ford Tempo. In her lap she holds a clipboard with the file of a new case she is investigating. She follows the directions to the house; knows the neighborhood well. The streets are lined with skinny, two-story houses all painted white with green trim; all the porches are identical with a single, cement block step painted grey. Many houses in the area nearby are condemned; windows covered with plywood.

Colleen walks across the street, looking down at her clipboard reviewing information about the case— the mother, her live-in boyfriend, the infant.

Walking up the step onto the porch, she notices a blue blanket hanging over the window like a drawn curtain; white lighthouses with red spiral stripes are patterned in rows right-side up and rows up-side down. All the tops are lit up with yellow light.

Colleen knocks on the storm door and waits on the porch, looking at the lighthouses. She knocks a few more times, but no one answers the door.

Colleen walks back to her car. Across the street from the lighthouses, a woman is sweeping her walk. She wears canvas sneakers and a long powder-blue sundress with tiny red, white and yellow flower graphics; her white hair rolled up into a ball on top of her head is held together with two pencils. She moves the broom over the walk, cleaning dirt and grass clippings. She looks up as Colleen reaches her car. She says, "He's in there, honey. Just not answering the door. The devil himself if I've ever seen him."

Colleen says thank you and opens the door. The woman smiles and says, "No. Thank you."

The elevator doors open. Colleen and Ricky walk in; Colleen's purse rests at her hip, the strap on her shoulders. Ricky looks at all the buttons with numbers on them. Colleen tells him to push number twenty-eight, it lights up, and Ricky feels his brain move into his belly.

Colleen and Ricky walk side by side through the hallway on the top floor of the courthouse building, passing offices, a water fountain and restrooms. A full length window at the end of the hallway stretches from the floor to the ceiling.

They walk up to the window and look down at the alley below, the parked cars and the dumpsters.

Holding hands, they walk back down the hallway to the stairwell door. Inside the stairwell, they walk up the half-flight to a door with a sign that reads: Roof Access—Keep Door Closed At All Times.

On the roof they see the four foot high wall and the floor perimeter. Stainless steel roof turbines spin. Looking beyond the wall—blue sky—the only other visible thing. Walking toward the wall, Colleen can see the buildings nearby—the sky—the east and west mountain chains that make up the Susquehanna Valley, and the towns that make up the North and South Valley areas.

Colleen scoops Ricky up around the waist with her left arm to show him Public Square directly below, its diamond-tilt with all the buildings and cars, trees, and people. Ricky rests his forearms on the ledge, smiles, and Colleen tells him that all the people look like little ants; he laughs at the idea. She points to the Public Square Bank, sitting directly between a department store and a drug store.

Colleen takes a red Superball out of her purse on her right hip. She shows it to him, holding it out over the wall, her elbow resting on the ledge. He smiles. She throws the Superball down to the ground with all the force she could.

The Superball falls like a waterfall, cascading past the dozens of floors, hitting the middle of the street directly below. It bounces about fifty feet high at its peak, rainbowing over Public Square, above trees and a fountain, landing in a grove at the far end of the diamond. It bounces off the grass a few feet, lands on the sidewalk, and rolls down Main Street out of sight.

Colleen parks the car. Two of her cats lying in the yard get up to stretch. She takes her files, computer, and cell phone, and walks up the walk to the back porch. The late afternoon sun is low and the branches move in and out of its way with the warm breeze. She greets the cats with a friendly, warm tone. Placing everything on the table, she calls for Greg as she walks to the bathroom. The house is quiet.

Walking into the bedroom to change clothes, she sees that the computer desk is clear of clutter; all of Greg's files, mail, and Post-It notes are gone. His pictures on the dresser and the one on the wall are gone, too.

In the living room she sees his guitar case and swivel rocker gone; all of his things are gone. She sits on the couch, her hands folded in her lap, staring at the wall; the afternoon light soft on the light-yellow walls.

Colleen continues to sit on the couch until long after the sun has set and it is dark, her hands folded in her lap, eyes open. As vehicles pass by the house, or turn at the corner, light from headlamps cuts into the windows through the darkness; reflections moving on the walls and ceiling appear in sharp-lined, erratic patterns.

The lobby in the Susquehanna County Courthouse is artificially lit along with the two large skylights in the ceiling. The grey marble and the oak trim are dulled by dense rain clouds. The overhead windows transit the scarce, grey light.

No afternoon highlights accent the oak baseboards, benches and stairs in the courthouse. No rays flecked with dust pass through the skylights to show the contrast between the browns and blacks, or the golds and ambers of the oak benches, and the trim.

Colleen sits on the bench, directly underneath the gray skylight; the sun is near its zenith, but invisible behind the clouds. She sits with her head down, unwinding the string in a figure eight pattern from the clasps on a file case.

He walks in wearing a navy-blue suit too small for him with white, tube-socks and brown shoes. His public defender sits on a bench across the lobby and continues his conversation on his phone while he just stands there waiting to be acknowledged.

Outside, the moon is passing between the Earth and the Sun. The clouds continue shifting over the valley; they block the view of the solar eclipse.

Susquehanna Valley

The moon has enveloped the Sun, briefly stopping light from shining into the atmosphere. Colleen's pupils dilate, adjusting to the darkening lobby. She looks up. The small lamp attached to the wall above the painting of the Iroquois over-looking the valley seems brighter than usual, contrasting the darkness. The people across the lobby are vague and out of focus, like an underexposed black and white photograph; specifics such as age, gender, hair color and height are lost to the darkening building, the darkening atmosphere. He continues to stand in the lobby.

Colleen turns to check the other lamps throughout the lobby, but they are all lit, and shining as bright as possible, like lighthouses in thick fog.

Colleen hears him clear his throat. He then says to his lawyer, "but the child is not mine."

Colleen finishes dressing in the living room. She keeps her leather jacket and chaps, helmet, goggles and gloves in the closet.

She walks back into the bedroom. Standing in front of the mirror, she turns herself around to see her butt and legs.

Opening the door to the garage, she sees her bike parked at the wall.

She pushes the bike out into the drive, throws her leg over the seat and straddles it. She fires the bike up and fixes her goggles and helmet. Sitting down, she winds the throttle, squeezes the clutch, and lets it out. By the time she reaches the end of the alley, she lifts her right leg onto the frame as she makes a left turn onto her street.

She heads west, onto a two lane state route leading out of the valley, up into the mountains. As she cruises along Harper's Creek, the temperature is a few degrees cooler; the road is shady; sunlight flashes through the leaves overhead.

A yellow motorcycle in the eastbound lane moves toward Colleen, heading down the mountains into the valley. The rider wears a denim vest; three eagle feathers fastened to his upper arm fly back in the breeze. The rider extends his entire left arm toward the ground at a forty-five degree angle, hand open, and fingers extended.

Colleen grins as she sees the rider's open hand, calling out to her, bouncing her like a Superball back into a world she had forgotten. She holds her arm out parallel to the ground, her fore and middle fingers extended, and signals back.

Gene Murray, 1911—2005

O*ctober, 1918*

Gene and his sister hold hands as they walk through town to Carroll's Market. She pulls him along; his little feet making the steps as quick as possible. Warm October breezes sway the yellow, orange and red leaves; some fly through the air and fall to the ground. Gene holds onto coins in his fist. Up ahead of them, their father and uncle push a hand-cart with their cousin Jimmy inside.

In the distance, across from the market, they could hear a cacophony of thin and hollow sounds— hammers on nails and hammers on boards, and saws cutting through lumber. A group of young men perform like carpenters outside the Landon Funeral Home, constructing boxes six feet long, three feet wide and one and one-half feet deep. Mounds of sawdust pile up on the brick sidewalk.

Townspeople arrive pushing wheelbarrows and hand carts, or they pull up in horse-drawn carts, wagons, and flat-beds; all filled with corpses—some still warm, most cooling and stiffening. The bodies had reached over one-hundred three degrees in peak fever, twitched in muscle ache and had been delusional; they then drowned in their own fluid.

People lay the corpses in rows on the porch, in the foyer, and out onto the tree lawn; in some places, they pile them on top of one another.

Volunteers fill completed coffins with corpses and label them; the young men hammer them shut—the tops not always flush to the sides, the slats on the bottoms not always square, none of the edges sanded smooth to touch.

Gene stands outside the market, watching the scene outside the funeral home; he watches his father and uncle speak to a man, shake hands with him and then place Jimmy, who recently turned seventeen, on the ground. He clutches the coins in his fist, watching and listening.

People on both sides of the street cover their mouths and noses with their arms. Gene feels his sister tug on his hand and begin to drag him into the market; he continues looking over his shoulder across the street at the boxes and the corpses, the hammering, the sawing, the ordinary people doing extra-ordinary things.

November, 1934
A few inches of snow cover the neighborhood. Gene walks out his backdoor and then down Carpenter Street in the dark; his feet crunching on the dry, flaky snow. The neighborhood is quiet. Smoke drifts from chimneys; his breath visible with each exhale. He

wraps himself up as best he can with his coat, carrying his lunch pail with a sandwich in the top compartment, another in the middle compartment and water in the bottom. He wears a canvas cap with his carbide lamp attached. Reaching the mine-track that runs east-west through the valley, he begins walking toward St. Christopher's field, a large, open field behind the church.

A cart makes its way down the track in the dark and Gene jumps on. They ride through town and reach the field, now the main entrance to the southeast mines in the valley. A large pit has been excavated with tracks leading down into the earth; a string of light bulbs suspended from the ceiling disappears into the darkness.

Lumber supports the sides and the top of the entrance. Dozens of men gather around the lights, standing in the snow. Snow flurries fly and the generators sound in the darkness. Tombstones covered with snow in St. Christopher's cemetery, adjacent to the field, stand like men waiting. The foreman calls off names from a clipboard. One by one, men walk away from the crowd and turn on their lamps. Gene steps off the cart, speaks to the foreman for a few minutes and descends into the mine; he hears the name of the last man, and knows that many men will be left in the dark, all without work for the day, some with lunches, some without; all with little hope.

Gene walks through town after a day in the mines. He carries a cut of pork wrapped in wax-paper.

Kerosene street lamps light the snow-driven cobble-stone road. The buildings are dark but block the wind.

Gene sees people standing in a line, bundled to protect from the cold; they shiver while they stand with their chins and cheeks tucked into their coats. The line extends down the block and around the corner.

A one and one-half ton truck with canvas covering the bed sits outside of Carroll's Market. Men in the back pass down boxes and bags filled with bread and other perishables. The shivering men in line accept the food and stick it into their coats as they walk away.

As Gene approaches the back of the truck, a man with an un-kept beard dressed in multiple layers of shirts takes the bread from a man's hands; he immediately takes a bite and begins chewing while walking. Men in line begin pushing and shoving other men—accusations of line-cutting, unfair portions and nepotism are made. A fight breaks out in line, and Gene can hear the hollow sound of fists striking cheeks, chins and eye-sockets; he places his package into his coat and continues walking home.

A few doors down from the market, a group of men sit on the sidewalk, leaning up against the brick of an apartment building; their knees at their chins, they wrap their arms around their shins to bundle themselves up. One man at the far end of the building is slumping up against the wall. A woman walking into the building tells him to get up off the cold ground; she nudges him a little and speaks to him again. He is unresponsive and silent; his torso leans a little closer to the ground.

Winter, 1940

Gene is the foreman of the Shoemaker Street mine in the north-west area of the valley, and directs the miners on their operations for the day. The men need good tools and equipment. Gene personally oversees that they receive fair prices for their product and makes sure they all have something to eat.

In the kitchen after dinner, Mary cleans the table around him. A single oil lamp lights the room, and a fire in the wood stove helps heat the downstairs. She talks to him about her day and about things going on with the neighbors, and relatives. Gene responds to Mary with few words and looks out the window to see a dog sniffing around the street; near the houses, a squirrel scurries along a grey limb toward the trunk carrying a chestnut and then disappears into a knot-hole. He smiles to see a family of four walking by on the sidewalk, the mother and father talk and the kids laugh together.

Mary continues washing and drying dishes and putting things away. Even though Gene is a little distant, she continues to talk. Sometimes he looks up to her, his eyes wide, head tilted; sometimes he blinks but usually nods to acknowledge her. Mary knows that men arrived to the Shoemaker St. mine entrance hoping to work for the day; she knows that Gene had to tell them he was sorry and that they walked away cold and nervous. Gene knows that their tables could have had more, that the children ate, but not well enough, and that the men are hungry, and afraid.

December, 1985

Palm trees and parking meters line the boulevard that runs parallel to the ocean two blocks east. A warm, off-shore breeze blows down the blocks of Fort Lauderdale that run perpendicular to the beach. Gene pulls into a parking spot at ten-forty five in the morning. The sun is warm; about as warm as it will be all day.

Mary gets out, opens up the rear passenger side door and begins collecting a chair, an umbrella and a small cooler. She wears a visor, sunglasses, and a light-weight sundress.

Groups of people make their way across intersections toward the horizon; they also carry chairs and other beach items.

Mary closes the doors on her side and waits on the sidewalk. Gene writes in a notebook, closes it shut and stuffs it under the driver's seat in his Caprice Classic. He closes and locks the door. He wears a pair of cut-off, stitched slacks, loafers and a short-sleeve, button-down shirt with the shirt tails un-tucked. As he walks by the parking meter, he can see that there are still thirty minutes left.

Summer, 2005

Gene worked as a 'Beans and Bullets' guy in France during the Second World War. He made sure that all the soldiers had everything they needed. The

CO for his company relayed to him their operations and all the logistics for those operations. Gene made sure that provisions were sufficient—tents, generators, kitchen staff and supplies, cots, blankets, medical staff and supplies, vehicles, weapons, ammunition, and clothing. He also provided extras—like footballs, baseball bats and balls, alcohol, and a film projector and screen.

He made sure that mail was delivered to, and sent from their AO; no matter how remote, or dangerous.

After the war, Gene worked as a civil engineer in the valley and the surrounding areas. He helped design the Cross-Valley Parkway, connecting the east and west valley over the Susquehanna River.

In 1952, Hurricane Eleanor moved in on the valley. She also hit the areas north into the Appalachian Mountains where the Susquehanna River headwaters lie. It rained for nearly two weeks straight.

All the creeks and rivers north of the valley flooded, and they all over-flowed into the Susquehanna River; it crested at thirty-four feet, but the water from the north continued to pour in, and then it rose up and over the levees and flooded the valley. Homes were underwater up to the second story. The water came over the levee with such force into St. Christopher's Cemetery, that caskets were up-rooted and then seen floating down Susquehanna Avenue. Gene worked through the 60s engineering the levee raising project. They raised it fifteen feet.

Days after Gene's funeral, his son and daughter, Mark and Jean-Marie, began to clean out the home, preparing to put it on the market. They hired a company to come and put a thirty square yard dumpster in the back yard.

Boxes packed tight with old clothes, dishes, and gadgets, piled from the floor to the ceiling in the basement; the junk filled the entire surface area except for a little path from the stairs to the washer and dryer. The garage and attic were identical—filled with boxes and stuff dating back to the old house on Carpenter Street before the move in the early 50s.

The house took months to go through. Mark and Jean-Marie put away keep-sakes for themselves; and then Mark got to the point one day where he was throwing un-opened, un-rummaged boxes out the attic window into the dumpster below.

In the dining room, Jean Marie packed boxes with books from the bookshelves that covered all the walls. She took trips to Goodwill with different household items. While working, she accidentally dropped a hard-covered book and a fifty dollar bill fell out onto the floor. She began opening up books and thumbing through their pages; she'd hold the front jacket with one hand, and the back jacket with the other, binding up, and let the pages flop around in between.

Jean-Marie found two-hundred fifty more dollars in the same box. Casey, her friend, who was helping to clean stuff out, said she'd heard of this happening before. They checked other places in the house—underneath mattresses, behind drawers, under loose floor boards and in pockets of old clothes.

After they had gone through all the books in the house, they started looking through the pockets of winter clothes in the closet; they found a roll of five-hundred dollars in one coat, and another roll of three-hundred fifty in another. By the time the dumpster had been taken away, painters, cleaners, and landscapers hired, Jean-Marie and Mark found over twenty-five hundred dollars stashed throughout the house.

Mark laughed at all the money hidden in the house. He reminded Jean-Marie about the Easter dinner a few years ago when Gene tipped the server only five percent on a two-hundred thirty dollar bill. Gene became furious when Mark tried to leave more money on the table. Even Mary said for Mark to leave it if he wanted to leave it. Gene stood by the table until Mark walked out of the restaurant in front of him.

Mark ended up living in the house for a few months after the funeral while they cleaned out the house. He drove Gene's Caprice Classic around from time to time to keep it running; it had a FOR SALE BY OWNER sign in the rear window. Under the driver's seat, Mark found Gene's notebook—a ledger of some sort—complete with months, dates, years, and various detailed columns with rows containing figures; one column was a cumulative total. The ledger was full from 1980 to 2004.

Each year began in the second week of November and ended in late April. The first was an arrival column—showing times early to late morning, sometimes early afternoon, and the second one for departure, usually late afternoon to early evening. Another column was just digits, which Mark deduced as the amount of hours between both times.

The next column was a dollar amount; the amounts averaged roughly the same for each day, ranging from two and one-half dollars to four dollars or so. The last column was a cumulative total.

Each month the total began anew. Monthly totals for the first few years averaged about ninety dollars; cumulative totals increased throughout the years. On random dates throughout the months and years, a ten dollar debit was subtracted from the total; this happened twice a month or so on average.

The daily and cumulative totals inflated throughout the years, as well as the random debits.

The day Mark found the ledger, he sat reading and flipping pages in the driveway with the engine running for nearly an hour until he figured out that it was all money saved from money not spent. He found a ten dollar parking ticket receipt from the Fort Lauderdale Police Department in the back of the journal. The date and amount of the receipt corresponded to a debit in the journal.

Mark shut the engine off, skipping the appointment with the Notary Public on the Avenue. He read the ledger while walking up the drive to the back porch. He walked in the back door, opened the fridge, pulled out a bottle of beer and sat on the back steps studying the ledger

He sat for a time on the back steps, looking out at the trees filled with birds and squirrels, thinking about the ledger and his father—the pack-rat, the horrible tipper who stashed money throughout the house; a man who saved over two-thousand dollars gambling with the Fort Lauderdale police for over twenty years. A man who saw his family die around him as a child, who watched his community almost perish as a young man, who fought with his brothers and neighbors. A man who worked his whole life for his community, for his family.

Mark smiled, opened another beer and then used his cell-phone to call Jean-Marie and tell her about the ledger.

Made in the USA
Lexington, KY
01 June 2012